G R JORDAN'S

Unravel Your Destiny

Darkness on a Foreign Shore

First published by Carpetless Publishing in 2019

First Edition

ISBN: 978-1-912153-51-0

Cover art by J Caleb Clarke

To all the heroes and heroines who work without credit but who continue so that the day does not become any darker

TABLE OF CONTENTS

Page

Dedication 3

Table of Contents 5

How to Play 7

Darkness on a Foreign Shore 11

The Author 328

Author Notes 330

A Small Request 332

Notes 333

How to Play

Hi and welcome to the first *Unravel Your Destiny* adventure, *Darkness on a Foreign Shore*, where you play as a female spy crossing the English channel to France during World War II to try to assist the resistance, arrange safe passage for other spies, sabotage the German forces and steal plans.

If you haven't experienced a gamebook where you make the decisions before, don't worry, it's easy to play but not so simple to win. You'll start at the paragraph numbered

001

and from there you move to other numbered paragraphs depending on your decisions. Make sure you hold your finger on the section you are moving from until you have reached the one you are moving to, in case you forget the number. Remember, your journey and the success of it depends on you. Your choices, your consequences and yours the glory if you can pull it off.

During the adventure you may collect items or outfits. Be sure to write these down in your **Notes** section at the rear of the book. Also these pages are good to write down any clues, codes, or important information you acquire. Better to rely on your pencil rather than your memory, although the real spies didn't have that luxury.

During some sections you may be required to work out codes that take you to a numbered paragraph. If that paragraph doesn't make sense then you are at the wrong one. Go back to the paragraph you came from and follow the instructions.

At times in the book you will be up against the clock and will need to record how many minutes you have at the start, and then how many are remaining as you deduct the time taken for your activities. The tabular chart at the rear in the **Notes** section will allow you to do this simply.

Please note there are no dice required for this book. Occasionally your decisions may be a matter of luck. If so, simply choose one of the numbers given to you. Not everything in life can be predicted or calculated, sometimes we just have to go on chance.

Certain choices mean you will end the mission and at this point you have a few options. You can return to the previous paragraph and choose another option. You can return to the main start point for that particular mission, these are usually numbered from **001** to **020**. Or you can do as the book suggests and go back to **001** and start all over again. Whatever you do, have fun!

Now get ready to go undercover in a foreign land as you prepare to start your mission. Remember you are the hero! You decide! And the best of British luck to you!

Let the adventure commence!

001

Well, this is it. All the training, all the learning, the tests and mental preparation comes down to this. As the waves lap the side of the dinghy, you let your eyes adjust to the dark, knowing you're on your own from here. No more get outs, no more trying the methods again, this time they have to work and work well, each and every time.

Standing on board the small naval vessel, you can barely remember your life when it was quiet and calm. A top student at school, your mother, an Englishwoman, had married an American and you had been born in London before moving to the United States. Your life had been a good one, with plenty of friends, sunny days and a happy life until your father's unfortunate car accident. Your mother struggled without him and you had returned home at the age of sixteen with a prime American accent and a solid education that you continued on your return.

But then 1939 came along and something happened that older generations had dreaded, war had begun. Now in your early twenties, you were enlisted into Bletchley Park with your cognitive reasoning skills. Impressing many people, you were approached to join Special Operations with the chance to serve in France. The war has been raging two years and after being held from British shores, the Germans remain in occupied France. It is there that you are to go and help the resistance.

You trained hard, learnt French and a little German but the key to your cover was always going to be that fantastic American accent you can turn on and off at will. Being a product of two countries meant you could change cover, a pre-requisite for any good spy.

And so you are headed to France to become a radio operator, taking in signals and arranging air drops, weapons movements, pilot rescue, infiltrations and espionage, all to help stop this German machine that has so quickly taken over much of Europe.

When you had left headquarters, everyone was so affirming if quiet. Too many operatives had never come back and their sacrifices, although appreciated, were always a blow to friends who had sent them away. Few knew where you would be going as secrecy was so important.

The car had taken you to the docks and you had been transferred to the vessel lying off the shore in the dead of night. After two days sailing holed up in a small bunk, you dressed in black clothing to face the trip to shore, and landing in France. There will be a contact to meet you on the beach and they will send a simple signal out to the dinghy to draw you in. But you know there are also patrols all over the beaches and this could be the trickiest part of your time in France.

The Naval Captain taps your shoulder and indicates it is time. Stepping down the rope ladder into the dinghy you have so little with you. With just a few French Francs, and little else in case you are captured, you will be dependent on your contact for papers and plans for the next stage. You need to get this right.

The Captain waves a silent farewell as his vessel slowly moves away from you and you can see the shoreline ahead. Taking the oars, you begin to row towards the beach, desperate to get off the slightly choppy sea and reach dry land. You were never a good sailor, and this tiny boat is making you a little queasy. Or maybe it's the risk you're taking that's affecting you.

Looking at the beach you can see lights. They appear to be swinging this way and that, and it's hard to see a message in what's being shown. Maybe it's the terrain that's causing the awkwardness, or maybe the visibility isn't great as you bob up and down. Or maybe that's not your contact. You could route further round the beach and come ashore at the rocks, but that would be dangerous especially in these choppy waters. You could head to other parts of the beach but again you don't know what is there. Headquarters were very specific about where on the beach to land. What do you do?

Route towards the lights to meet up with them on the beach – goto **021**

Move your dinghy away from the lights – **141**

Abandon the boat and swim for it – **061**

002

The cupboards range right round the kitchen disappearing under the sinks. Inside you find a series of different crockery items and cutlery, but nothing of significant interest. However at the side of one of the cupboards, you can see a key chain with a range of keys. You may pocket them if you wish, **decide now**.

Otherwise you can find nothing else you can make use of. You close all the doors of the cupboards and think about your next move. If you haven't before, do you,

Investigate the dumb waiter – **042**

Check out the storeroom – **082**

Exit the kitchen – **200**

Or if you are still wearing your German outriders uniform goto **022**

003

The days seem to all roll into one as you work your radio in the evenings, passing on messages from London and sending back vital information. But there is little else to do except work on the farm. Although summer days are hot and there is sweet local fruit to eat, there is always the fear of discovery hanging over your head and the inaction makes you feel vulnerable.

Then one night, you receive from London an urgent message advising that a prime asset has been captured and is held locally. However, he is to be moved the very next night by train, courtesy of the Gestapo, to Germany. You have orders to stop that transfer and then to rescue the prisoner from the local detention area before helping to return him to England.

Your hands shake as you decode the message given but inside a flame is ignited. This is why you signed up, to be a part of something special, and this mission is certainly that. Despite the fear that also comes with this kind of message, you find courage in thinking of the service you will do your country.

You arrange for a meeting of the resistance heads and detail the message received to them. There is little time to organise and you spend most of the night thinking through plans and examining the timetable of the train you have been given.

A train will be coming into the town and picking up the prisoner at the main station. To do that it will come in on a single line and that line has to cross a bridge, then go past a remote section near the woods and then arrive through the town to the station. You discuss these three areas and which to attack in order to send the train back. The bridge is exposed unlike the wood. The station will be crawling with Germans but is where the train will be static. The woods are close to town whereas the bridge requires a detour of almost twenty miles if not used across insecure ground for the Germans.

In the end the heads decide that the decision of where to destroy must be made on the night, according to troop movements and other variable factors. To facilitate this decision, you will initially rendezvous at a small house on the edge of the river, close to the bridge. From here all three sites will be accessible. Also here you will pick up the required explosives to stop the train. You have had training in using these explosives and for that reason you will be going along and advising on the site to use.

The next day flies along and you manage to catch some sleep in the afternoon in order to be at your most alert that night. Departing, you get onto a cart while the sun is still setting. You pick up various members of the resistance and hide them in the hay on the back of the cart. Not expecting any trouble in reaching the house, you are shocked to see a Gestapo vehicle coming the opposite direction.

On seeing you, it pulls over and then starts to follow your cart. The driver of the cart looks at you and suggests you pull over. You have alternative papers tonight and a different disguise but they are as yet untested. You could simply pull over. Or you could keep going, after all why make an encounter when one is not needed. Do you,

Tell the driver to keep moving on - **023**

Tell the driver to pull over and await the Gestapo – **043**

004

After sleeping through the morning and early afternoon, you are wakened and taken to the barn where the radio set is kept. Some of the local resistance are there with some hand drawn maps of the barracks where the prisoner is being held. There are simply too many German soldiers there to mount an attack and it has been decided that you will need to smuggle the prisoner out. In order to do this you are going to disguise yourself as a maid and enter the barracks inside the laundry when the other maids are admitted in the evening.

This plan fills you with more than a little trepidation as you will be on your own from the moment you enter the barracks and you don't know the detail of the barracks that well. Some maps have been sketched from those loyal Frenchwomen who work there but this will be no easy task.

As you brush your hair in preparation for your task tonight, you find yourself recalling all the work put into learning your spy craft back at base in England. Over there it seemed easier, less deadly but now the stakes are for real. London must think this prisoner a very important asset to risk such an operation.

You cycle over to the far side of town and rendezvous with a local resistance fighter who introduces you to the maids who will carry you inside in a laundry basket. They look solemn and very apprehensive as you are loaded into the basket and covered with white linen. As best as they can tell the prisoner is being held in a building that houses the Commander of the barracks and also the cells. The maids have never been inside but they will be able to drop you close by when they enter the compound to go about their tasks.

All around you is dark as you feel yourself being lifted in the basket and then you are loaded onto a van. As the vehicle bounces along the road, you find yourself thrown this way and that and feel somewhat sick. After what seems like an age, you hear a German voice speak in French asking for papers and you believe the van has arrived at the compound. The van then moves forward again before coming to a halt and the engine switches off.

You hear the back doors open and you feel yourself swinging slightly as you are carried. You know you will be dropped right beside an entrance to the main building but you don't know which one as this decision will have to be made by seeing the positions of guards at the time. And then comes the signal as a quiet whisper and a tap on the laundry bring you to life. Your eyes are hit by the amount of light suddenly available.

You stand up and step out of the basket, seeing a wooden door straight ahead. You appear to be in a rear yard of the building and the maids are already carrying the basket they transported you in off in a different direction. You cannot hang around and so you open the door before you and step inside.

Goto **024**

005

It's a late summer evening when you are on the radio to London and receive an urgent message detailing a request to steal German plans from a chateau approximately one hundred miles away. From the detail received you believe this will be a difficult mission and you have been requested to undertake it and bring the plans back by hand to England.

Part of you is nervous about such a mission but there is also a part of you delighted to have a chance at getting back to England. You know it will take a good deal of organising and that success is not guaranteed. However, you first contact the local resistance asking for help with surveillance on the chateau and ideas for how to get into the building.

According to HQ, they think the plans will be located in the offices of a Brigadier General Klaus Hauser but the exact location within his suite of offices is unknown. There are no insiders at the chateau as far as you know at this time and entry may be difficult. Moving around as a German soldier would seem the best idea.

When it is one week out from the go date for the mission, you say goodbye to the owner of the farmhouse, wondering if you will ever see her again. The base has served you well but you will be glad when you can walk down a street once again without thinking you could be stopped at any moment and potentially shot.

You travel at night by car along back roads and via mountain roads to a spectacular village in the mountains. Here you are hidden in the roof space of a town house and are given plans and photographs of the chateau. Although you are able to memorise the shape and orientation of the rooms, you will not know exactly what awaits you in every room. This is a large risk and London must believe these plans are worth it. All you know is they are called Operation Snow Hammer.

The days roll by and you are informed by the local resistance that they have captured a German side car and a uniform which they will adjust to your size. The uniform is female and one of the German auxiliary types which suits the female role. However to get you into the chateau, you will be wearing an outriders jacket and helmet along with false I.D. This should get you up to the chateau itself and not stopped at the outer ring of buildings that sit a level below.

It is known that several female auxiliaries serve in the chateau and as long as you keep on the move you should be able to pass yourself off as one of these. But you will also need guile and luck to move to the General's suite and acquire the plans. For this reason you will be going into the chateau after midnight with the aim to leave in darkness as well.

The day comes and you try to sleep in the afternoon but you are troubled by nerves and trepidation. When you rise, evening has set in and you eat a good meal to prepare yourself. It may be a long while before you eat again. If you escape the chateau with the plans you will need to get to the coast and rendezvous with a Royal Navy gunship which will take you to Southampton.

When darkness falls you dress in your axillary uniform and then don the outrider's jacket, helmet and googles. Your skirt is hitched up over your trousers and tucked into the jacket making you looking chubbier than you are. A car arrives and takes you to a barn on the outskirts of the town. Here you are shown the sidecar and you wonder what it will be like to ride it. You have ridden motorbikes in the past but this will be a bit different. After familiarising yourself with the controls you head out of the garage, headlamp lighting up the road as the hour approaches midnight.

This is it, a mission you will come back from a hero or not at all. These next few hours could be your last and they will be some of the most traumatic of your life. Good luck!

Goto **025**

006

You have the plans and now you need to leave quickly and begin your journey to England. Your first task is to escape the chateau and with that in mind you think about your escape options.

You could simply walk down the stairs and bluff your way past the guard before exiting in the normal way, and then find your sidecar to depart in. But there may be other options.

Have you seen the dumb waiter in the "Meeting Room" – **026**

Did you look in the ottoman in the General's bedroom – **046**

Did you take the chloroform from the bathroom – **106**

If you did none of these, or have thought through the ones that apply to you, goto **126**

007

The Gestapo officer looks at you questioningly. "I wonder if you should have known a little more than that." You go to answer but it appears he is mulling over his decision and he puts a finger to his lips indicating you should be quiet. He looks at your papers even closer now.

Are you lucky?

Maybe try **047**

Or try **067**

008

You take the key and try it on the cell door. It opens and you decide you need to brief the man on what to do next. But he doesn't give you a chance. Instead he bolts past you and straight out into the corridor. Soon you hear a commotion and there are guards everywhere searching the building. Although you manage to leave the cells you are caught trying to secret yourself in the building.

You are taken to a prison by a van and are interrogated. For three months you endure daily questions and methods of persuasion that cause you great pain. But then one morning you are taken outside in the first rays of sun and positioned beside a wall and given a blindfold to wear. You hear a squad of soldiers being told to ready, aim and then fire. And then your war is over.

You have failed. Did you go off mission? Try again at 001.

009

You walk towards the beggar who seems very drunk. His clothes stink and you wonder how someone could have produced such a good disguise. Surely this is just an old drunk. He lounges around but on seeing you pats the grass beside him and tries to get you to sit down with him. Do you,

Sit in silence beside him – **212**

Talk out loud to the beggar – **049**

Leave the beggar and if you haven't already, talk to the old woman (**358**), the German soldier (**298**) or the peasant man (**418**)

010

Is the British airman running a diversion for you – **030**

If not – **050**

011

Opening the door, you see the inside of a bathroom with a small bath in the corner, a cabinet above a wash basin, a toilet at the far wall with a window above it and a small black case on the floor. A uniform hangs on the back of the door. (*Deduct 1 min if this is your first time at 011*). Do you,

Examine the bath - **031**

Take a look at the toilet and window - **051**

Check out the cabinet and wash basin - **071**

Look at the small black case on the floor - **091**

Search the uniform on the back of the door - **111**

Or if there is nothing of interest to you return to **213** and choose another option

Or has time gone for you, in which case - **376**

012

You don't hang around and immediately open up the window at the rear of the room and climb out onto a small ledge. Shutting the window behind you, you carefully make your way down across smaller roofs with your case. Your dress gets torn and your shoes become scuffed but you are intact as you reach the bottom.

You are now in a small alleyway. Walking to the end of it, you can see the Germans watching the hotel and the arrival of a car, out of which steps a German officer. The same German officer who spoke to you at the station.

You immediately move off while they are focused on the hotel, walking at pace away from this part of the town, towards the river and the bridge you need to be at for your rendezvous.

Goto **271**

013

The soldier comes close to you and you hold your breath as best you can. He pulls away one case after another, throwing them aside and you feel the sweat drip into your eyes and sting them. But you don't flinch, your very life depends on it. His hand goes to the side of you and then he simply moves on to another case just across from you.

But then he thinks again and sweeps back towards you. You try to move your body out of the way but the case you are behind falls and you crash out to the front of the rack. You try to get up and run but are grabbed and taken to a van behind the station. Here you are blindfolded and go on a road journey before being flung into a prison cell somewhere unknown.

Daily, you are taken for torture and questioning but you have nothing to reveal. Once they realise this, you are taken one afternoon to a room where you see a guillotine. Within a minute you are dead, another fallen soldier on a different battle field.

You have failed, I guess your luck didn't hold. You can see if you are more fortunate next time by going to 001 and starting again. Of course real spies don't get that second chance.

014

You drag your escapee with you and make your way to the east gate. You had hoped that in the confusion of escape there would be few guards on this side gate but there seems to be a lot there today. This makes your subsequent capture fairly easy. You are taken away and placed in a van with a bag over your head.

After a short journey, you are deposited into a cell and the bag removed. This turns out to be your home for the next three months as you are interrogated. Every day there are questions and pain until one bright morning you are lead to a wall in a field and face a squad of German soldiers. This is where your war ends, another hero lost in a foreign field.

You have failed. Bit of bad luck there. Try again at 001.

015

As you walk past, the telephone operator asks you where your shoes are. You look down remembering that you took them off at the top of the stairs. Do you,

Run out of the door – **225**

Look embarrassed and say you left them in the General's quarters – **486**

016

You retreat back to the landing and focus on the other two doors. Which one will you approach next?

Do you enter the Guard room – **096**

Try your luck at the Commandant's Office – **235**

017

You go downstairs and ask the guard to come up and help you enter the room. When he gets to the top of the stairs and realises that you are trying to gain access to the General's office, he points his gun at you and asks you to accompany him downstairs. He says no one has access to that room except the General and that is a standing rule. You have no reason to be there and he suspects you are a spy. He takes you at gunpoint to the front of the building where he finds additional guards.

You are covered with a hood and find yourself next in a cell. For days you are questioned and tortured, giving up many secrets. After three months you are led away to a wall in a garden where you are shot by firing squad. Your last memory is the sound of birds chirping their morning calls, then rudely interrupted by the crack of gunfire.

You have failed. You actually asked the enemy for help? Goto 001 to try again.

018

You move the mechanism and it descends down the chute, taking the plans and dirty crockery to the kitchen below. You then casually walk to the stairs and descend them, telling the guard below that you are finished. He says that all personnel leaving the General's quarters are subject to search and you offer no resistance. You happily stand while he frisks you. After a few moments he stands back, satisfied, and waves you on your way. You route to the kitchen and take the plans from the dumb waiter.

If you stored your outrider gear in the kitchen cupboard you take it out again and dress in it. It's time to escape the chateau compound.

Did you read the electrical plans in meeting room – **055**

If not, where is your sidecar parked?

In the barn – **254**

Hidden in the trees in the orchard – **274**

019

You have arrived at a farmhouse with several large barns in the vicinity. As you are taken inside the house, chickens mill about your feet clucking their annoyance at your intrusion. Inside the building, the man from the hotel introduces you to a woman named Michelle and then simply wishes you all the best before leaving. His name is never given and you are unlikely to ever see him again.

Michelle is a formidable woman, almost six foot tall and with an enormous build. She looks slightly overweight but has strong arms and hands which she wipes on her apron. After sitting you down she fetches you some water and a loaf of bread with some cheese. You thank her and start to eat.

Michelle steps outside and looks like she is checking the area as she walks around the farmyard with the hens chasing after her. A dog then runs up to her and she brings it inside, pointing you out to the dog and then announcing you as a friend to it.

"We are alone," she says. "If anyone comes the dog and the hens will let me know. It is good to have a radio operator again. Later I will show you the barn where we keep it and where you shall sleep. Your cover whilst here is as a farm labourer, a mute girl that I have taken in for the summer. If you speak you will give away your nationality as they said your French was good but your accent wouldn't fit in as local. So you shall stay mute in company lest they discover you."

You can see disadvantages to that but you nod as the cover has been prepared for you.

"I am told you are a trained operative and that you are capable of taking on various missions but your main job will be to run communications between ourselves and London. You have arrived at a busy time, and our last radio operator was sadly killed during a night operation. She wasn't living here and the equipment was not here then so you need not worry that they will be looking here."

Michelle continues, talking about daily duties on the farm you need to be doing as well to complete your cover and then asks you to go and change your clothing. She indicates a small bedroom off the main hallway of the farmhouse and you find a mottled skirt and blouse and more run down clothing in a wardrobe.

After you change, she takes away all of your travelling clothes and suggests you clean the makeup off your face. The tour of the farm then starts including taking you to the radio and showing you the code books required to understand the messages London sends. You are familiar with using these and are excited to begin your mission properly.

After dinner, you spend some time in the dark of the barn calling London and receiving messages which you note down with pencil and paper. You fold each one up and mark it with a letter for the owner. Later a boy calls at the farm and takes the messages away.

For two weeks you work on the farm and decode messages at night. Most of the messages are routine and some talk about local troop movements. There are also messages to pass to London. Then one night you receive a message about the arrival of a spy, one who is required quickly and who is being dropped in by parachute.

The next day Michelle advises that you will be accompanying some resistance fighters in setting up the drop zone for the arrival of the new spy and also the subsequent moving on of the spy. Your blood pumps fast at the news and your heart skips a beat. At last you will be out on a real mission.

Goto **039** to start your mission

020

You tell him that you have work assigned by the General that needs completed by the morning. He seems dubious and asks you what work it is. You tell him it's for the General and obviously you can't discuss it, not that you understand most of it anyway. He laughs and talks about how we are all in the dark really. You laugh back and he waves you on through. Do you?

Walk on through the entrance hall – **379**

Talk to the switchboard operator – **180**

021

Dipping your oars back into the water, you press on towards the shore, making for the lights ahead. As you get closer to the beach and the waves start to break, you find the water very choppy and are thrown about.

As you glance over your shoulder, a touch of moonlight catches one of the figures on the beach in profile and you see the shape of a German uniform. You are stuck in rough water and surely getting out of the boat would be a risk, but there are also German soldiers on the beach. Where is your contact? You are too close in to turn the dinghy around, the breakers are carrying you in. What will you do?

Abandon the vessel -**161**

Take your chances on the beach with the German soldiers -**041**

022

You may change into your auxiliary uniform here and stow your outrider's jacket and trousers in the back of a cupboard at this time if you wish. But note it is hidden in the kitchen cupboards.

If you haven't before do you,

Investigate the dumb waiter – **042**

Check out the storeroom – **082**

Exit the kitchen – **200**

023

You whisper to the driver to keep moving and he gently urges the horse onward. The Gestapo car follows you, sitting back just a little. They are trailing you and you wonder how far they will do it. If they stay with you, you won't get to the explosives and the train will fetch its prisoner and the mission will have failed. You need to take action.

Do you race away in an attempt to lose them – **202**

Do you stop and let the Gestapo talk to you – **222**

024

Opening the door you find yourself at the end of a corridor. The walls are painted plain white and you get the feeling that this is a rear entrance for staff like yourself. Creeping along the corridor, you come to a flight of stairs heading up to the next floor and also two other hallways. One seems to lead to the front of the building and there is a significant degree of noise from that direction. The other leads to the rear of the building and you can see a sign in German saying "cells". Given the size of the building, there must be more than cells that way. Upstairs might contain the rooms of the Commander of the barracks and other important rooms as this is the central building.

You should not hang about but you need to decide where to go. Do you,

Climb the stairs – **144**

Route along the corridor to the rear part of the building – **044**

Investigate the noises coming from the front of the building – **064**

025

You ride along the road to the chateau, with the hills around you looming up on either side. The Germans must believe themselves safe to run their plans this high up and away from the general population. It has long been suspected the chateau is a major communications post and planning station but no one has ever gotten inside to confirm or deny this. Tonight you will, but will anyone find out the result from you?

The rain has begun and you wipe the googles as they begin to be peppered with droplets. Your hair is tied up under your outrider's hat and you try to lift your shoulders up to give as masculine a perception as possible. This may be one of the trickiest parts of the mission, simply getting in.

When you see the chateau, it is an impressive sight and you are amazed at the outer wall, nearly ten feet high, surrounding the entire grounds. You know that inside there is an orchard and some splendid gardens as well as a number of buildings. You ride up in your sidecar and approach the gate. Do you,

Wave at the gate guard as if you know him – **045**

Pull out your papers at the gate, a standard practice according to the local resistance – **165**

Simply stop and wait for someone to approach – **185**

026

You could put the plans in the dumb waiter and send them downstairs thereby walking past the guard at the foot of the stairs without them. Surely the guard will search you when you leave, and if he does you will be caught red handed. This is a plan worth considering. Go back to **006** and see if you have any other options before deciding.

027

You don't want to antagonise the officer and so you just stay quiet and hope that he will mutter on to himself about your papers. He takes a good, hard look at them now and then mutters something quickly in German to the captain that you cannot catch. You turn to smile at the friendly German but he now has a face that looks like thunder and he takes you by the arm, hauling you from the carriage and to the clutches of the Gestapo. From there you are taken to a prison and spend your few remaining days being tortured and questioned.

You failed. Better to be American than just stay quiet. If you want to try again goto 001.

028

You enter the room marked boiler and find a large boiler and pipework for a heating system. There's a small coal supply as well and you realise that this building is a converted family mansion. But enough of the history lesson and you look around for something useful. In front of the boiler on the ground is a piece of paper that looks like it's been scrunched up, possibly for the fire. There's also a German uniform hanging up, apparently drying. At the side of the boiler is a shovel. Do you,

Look at the paper on the floor – **048**

Grab the shovel for a closer examination – **068**

Take the German uniform down – **088**

029

You look at the safe and see it has three dials in a row, each one capable of setting a two digit number. The tumble dials seem easy to set up and there's a handle that needs to be turned to open the safe but at present it will not budge. (*If this is your first look at the safe you have spent 1 min examining it.*)

Do you want to try the tumble locks - **174**

Otherwise return back to **416** and choose another option

Or has time gone for you, in which case - **376**

030

As you get closer you see a man running amok and calling the Germans towards him. You recognise the British voice. Many of the Germans are leaving their positions. When you get to the west gate don't choose **090 or 110**

Goto - **050**

031

You get down on your hands and knees and look inside the bath but find it to be a typical washing facility. You dare not try the taps but instead run your hands under the bath and find only dust. (*Deduct 1 min for this search*)

Return to **011** and pick another option

Or has time gone for you, in which case – **376**

032

You turn into an alley and begin to open your case, quickly removing the plans from it. As you fumble through your papers, you sense someone watching and a voice tells you to stand up. You have been watched more closely than you realised and as soon as they saw you take the papers out they moved in.

You are taken to a prison where you are questioned and tortured for three weeks. Then one day you are taken out in the early morning sunshine with a firing squad. In the glorious early dawn you become another fallen hero on a foreign field.

You have failed. Bad idea to take your prize out in public. Try again at 001.

033

Together you walk out of town, still with your shopping basket. As you get out onto the road, clear of the town buildings you begin to feel a little relief. This is short lived as a German car and van pull up alongside you. A smart young German officer gets out and asks you in decent French if you are lost. You raise your hands, keeping up your role of being a mute, but your colleague answers that sometimes she gets confused being so old.

The officer demands your papers and you hand them over. He studies them carefully before coming up close to you. His glare is off putting but you don't flinch. He then pulls down the head scarf of your colleague and a rush of dirty brunette hair emerges, much younger than that which would adorn any older woman's head.

You are taken into the van and a hood is placed over your head. That is the last you see of your new arrival or indeed of anyone, other than Germans. In the remaining days of your life you are questioned before being shot one morning as the drizzle forms around the prison where you were kept.

You have failed. Maybe it's better to stick with plans once made. Try again at 001.

034

You drag your escapee with you and make your way to the west gate. There seems to be few guards about, however there is still a reasonable number to get past. Given your escapee's state you are going to need a bit of luck to succeed.

Did you start a fire as a diversion in the boiler room – **054**

If not -**010**

035

You say goodnight to the staff at the front desk and walk calmly out of the building. So far so good but now you need to get to your sidecar, or maybe you have an extra surprise to help you escape. If you took the electrical plans from the Meeting Room table then goto **055**.

If not, where did you park your sidecar?

In the barn – **254**

Hidden in the trees in the orchard – **274**

036

You quickly open the cupboards around the kitchen and find a myriad of equipment. Bowls, colanders, plates and cups are all evident as well as a number of aprons. However you also find a number of mouse droppings behind a large stack of plates and you can smell that mice have been all over the cupboard. You resolve not to eat any food here.

There seems to be nothing of note in the cupboards and with a chef knocked out on the floor you had better get moving back to the main objective. Do you,

Do you enter the Guard room - **096**

Try your luck at the Commandant's Office - **235**

037

Do you have 3 coloured keys, blue, green and yellow - **057**

If not, or you only have a few of the coloured keys, you try the locks and the door but it is still holding. You obviously don't have the necessary keys required. (*This attempt has taken you 2mins so deduct that from your time.*)

Go back to **479** and try another option.

Or has time gone for you, in which case - **376**

038

You try the mechanism and it's stuck. Nothing seems to make it budge. Maybe there's something downstairs that needs to be done. But you can't afford to hang about. Goto **126** and choose another plan.

039

In the dark of night you are sat in a ditch with four men, all of you dressed in black garb and awaiting the moment to step out and illuminate a drop zone for a parachutist. Marcel, the resistance leader, has led you to co-ordinates in the countryside that you provided on the radio just over a day ago. It should be a routine operation but there is always the chance that things can go wrong. You noticed a high presence of German troops about today on the road near the farmhouse and you began to get a little nervous. But now having arrived on scene with no issues, you are feeling confident and happy with everything that is happening.

You found out that day that one of the resistance men had been captured and that is why you needed to assist on the mission. Maybe that accounts for the increased German troop movements. Either way, you feel the excitement growing as you can hear an aeroplane in the distance, a little way off. It is on time.

As the four of you step out to begin to wave torches into the air to show the landing spot, you hear dogs and movement close by. There are lights approaching, still a little way off but they seem to be heading in this direction. Marcel seems worried. It is confusing as the lights are some way off and maybe the sound of the plane is what has the dogs barking. Or maybe the Germans have realised what is going on. Maybe the resistance has been tracked tonight.

Marcel seems frozen, unsure what to do. You know you cannot simply stand there and that a decision needs to be made. You could ward the aeroplane off with the abort signal which would mean the parachutist would drop at a nearby site and meet you at an alternative rendezvous point. You could just continue with the plan if you think the Germans are nothing to be worried about. Or you could cause a diversion, allowing the parachutist to land here while some of the mission team distract the Germans. What will you do?

Continue with the plan and indicate the drop zone is ready – **079**

Cause a diversion to send the dogs and Germans in another direction and allow the parachutist to continue – **099**

Send the abort signal to the aeroplane as it passes overheard and route to alternative Rendezvous point – **059**

040

You ask in a shy voice if are you in the right place for auxiliaries. The soldier smiles at you, obviously delighted that his dull shift has been broken up by someone. He says you are and asks to see your papers. You show him your documents and you notice he barely looks at them. When he has finished with the papers, he hands them back and asks what you will be working at. Do you,

Tell him you don't really know but are here for basic help – **060**

Tell him you've been requested by the General to complete some work – **080**

041

The waves throw the small dinghy this way and that as it runs for shore. You can see the lights just along from you and they begin to swing out. There are calls for you but you are too busy controlling the dinghy so you don't make the translation in your head, but they are definitely German. As the dinghy finally hits low water and begins to beach, you leap from it and begin to splash ashore. But there are lights around your feet. Then a voice calls out in French, telling you to wait. You keep running and it calls out again. But you continue to run. You hear the bullet being fired and then you are pitched into the sand. There's pain flowing through your body and you know you are doomed. Spies are never treated well and you can expect torture. At least you don't know anything to tell them yet.

You failed. Try again by returning to 001

042

You walk over to the dumb waiter and realise that it is in the up position and that the miniature lift for the food must be upstairs at the moment. Inside there's a small handle which seems to have locked the rope mechanism that allows it to travel up and down. Maybe it has been secured for the night. There's little else inside the device and you can imagine how it is used to send food up and down to someone important upstairs. Do you,

Want to release the handle – **062**

Leave the dumb waiter and if you have not done so

Search the cupboards – **002**

Check out the storeroom – **082**

Exit the kitchen – **200**

043

You tell the driver to pull over and await the Gestapo car's reaction. After a few moments, it pulls up alongside you and a Gestapo officer, dressed in his threateningly black uniform, looks the cart over closely. Then he walks to the front. Your driver starts to speak but he tells him to be quiet in French. Then he looks directly at you and asks, in English, "Are you enjoying your stay in France?"

Your heart pounds but you try not to show any emotion. But as you sit there you realise that the silence is making this more and more like a prepared reaction and so you must do something quickly. Do you,

Look forward like you don't understand – **063**

Reply in English – **143**

Complain about being examined in French – **163**

044

You take the corridor to the rear of the building and find there are three doors along it. One is locked and clearly says "Cells" on it in German. There appears to be a lock in the door and when you try to open the door it doesn't budge. You will need a key to gain access apparently.

The other rooms also are marked. One says "Boiler" and the other "Store". Both doors are slightly ajar indicating that they can be accessed.

Do you,

Enter the room marked "Boiler" – **028**

Enter the room marked "Store" – **148**

Retreat back to the stairs and climb them – **144**

Retreat back to the front corridor if you have not been that way before – **064**

Or do you think you have something which can get you access to the Cells – **164**

045

The gate guard holds a questioning hand up before coming over to you. He looks at you intently before asking you to remove your googles in German. You comply and he looks at you carefully. He asks if you have been here before. Do you,

Say yes, many times – **065**

No, never – **085**

Once – **105**

046

The ottoman in the General's bedroom had sheets in it which makes you think that you could tie them together and scale down the outside of the house. But you will need a window leading down to a suitable roof as the sheets were not that long.

If you have looked out of the bathroom window – **066**

If you haven't – **086**

047

You see the doubt in the eyes of the Gestapo officer but he's also under pressure from the German Captain. Eventually he concedes under duress from a senior officer and hands your papers back to you. The train continues its journey and you talk with the obliging Captain.

Goto **206**

048

You bend down and grasp the paper. It is written in German but fortunately that is a well-studied language for you. The scrap has writing that details the guard movements on the perimeter and it is dated yesterday. Maybe they will be the same today, or maybe not. You wonder if this piece of paper is useful but decide to pocket it anyway

The boiler suddenly makes a growling sound and you have no idea what that means. The shovel looks recently used and you decide you cannot hang about in case someone comes.

Leaving the boiler room you wonder what to do next. Do you,

If you haven't already, enter the room marked "Store" – **148**

Retreat back to the stairs and climb them – **144**

Retreat back to the front corridor if you have not been that way before – **064**

Or do you think you have something which can get you access to the Cells – **164**

049

You ask does he have much wine, in French, and he passes you some more. You start to enquire if he needs any help but he just keeps talking about the weather and moaning. You decide that you need to find out if he really is your contact and so you ask if he was ever in Switzerland. He nods and says he was always fond of Bern when he had money. Your heart pounds. Have you found your arrival? Do you,

Start advising him to come with you and that he is safe – **069**

Think it over and decide that you really forced the issue and this might be a trap – **089**

050

With your prisoner in tow this is going to be a real bit of luck to run past the guards. If you are running diversions then they may work but who knows. Choose one of the following:

070, 090, 110 or **130**

051

The toilet with its high cistern looks solid enough and you manage to look inside that tank by standing on the toilet. Unfortunately there is nothing but water and the plumbing mechanism inside. Disappointed by the toilet, you look out of the window beside it by peering behind the curtain, and find that there is a small drop to a flat roof below. From there you can just about make out another short drop to the ground. This may be a good escape route if you have something to lower yourself down with. (*Deduct 2 mins for this search and deduction*)

Return to **011** and choose another option

Or has time gone for you, in which case - **376**

052

You make for the nearest bar and enter to find a quiet affair with some tables occupied by German soldiers and a few locals. You see a table at the rear and slip into it awaiting the waiter to take your order. You ask for a glass of red wine and he nods before returning to get your drink. Out of the window you can see the people who were tailing you, watching and waiting. You are somewhat trapped and unable to go and meet your contact with this amount of heat following you. Do you,

Take the plans from the case and try to leave via the ladies toilets - **072**

Wait it out at the bar - **092**

053

You feel relieved when you turn into the farmyard where you live and your boss comes out to help the old woman inside. She takes her through to the barn and up into the loft where you have your radio equipment. There the old woman undresses and changes into a smart pair of trousers and blouse, ready for her next journey. She's a brunette, young, and very smart looking, completely different from the disguise she had employed up to this stage. You don't ask her name but you do bid her a fond farewell that night when the car comes to take her away.

You may not have known her name, or even where she comes from, but this is a small win in the war and you celebrate that in your head. Life returns back to normal, monitoring communications and passing messages but another mission will not be that far away.

Find out what it is at **003**

054

This has made the numbers at the gate even fewer as you see any soldiers run towards the house. When asked don't choose number **070**

Is the British airman running a diversion – **030**

If not - **050**

055

From the plans you scanned earlier you know that if you get to the main switchbox at the rear of the chateau you can effectively pull the plug on all the electrics and have the compound in total darkness. This could be invaluable for your escape and you carefully work your way around the building to the electrical shed at the rear.

The shed is effectively a large room with all the electrical feeds coming into the chateau emerging from the ground at this point. From a bush nearby you watch a guard patrol past and then time until the next one follows. There is a gap of five minutes.

As one guard leaves you race into the shed and pull the diagrams from your pocket. Looking along the panels in the shed, you identify the main intake and with a large tug on a handle you cut off the power into the chateau grounds. Before you run you start pulling fuses from boxes in the hope that if they switch it back on they will struggle to fix everything at once.

As you come out of the shed you bump into an auxiliary, who looks shocked to see you out here and asks what you are doing?

Are you in an outrider's outfit – **075**

Are you in an auxiliary's outfit – **175**

056

Taking a quick scan of the surfaces you find that this chef is not that tidy and there are bits of caked flour and sugar all over the rear of the surfaces. A number of knives have been left out amidst treacle stains and generally you are pretty disgusted by the general hygiene of the kitchen. But at the back of one of the surfaces, you notice what looks like a toothpick except that it's made of metal. It's a lock picking tool and one which you had the pleasure of using during your training. Generally good on older locks it was the basic tool that you learnt your lock picking skills on. It might come in useful so you pocket it.

With a chef lying on the floor you decide you need to keep moving and need to check out the other rooms on this top floor. Do you,

Do you enter the Guard room – **096**

Try your luck at the Commandant's Office – **235**

057

The keys turn easily in their respective locks. (*Take 1 min off your time.*)

Open the door and look inside – **416**

Or has time gone for you, in which case – **376**

058

You make your way from the hallway to the kitchen and head for the outside door. There's no one about and if you stored your outrider suit in the kitchen cupboard, you take this chance to put it on. You know that the best chance of escape is to get back into your sidecar and leave the way you came as they will have seen you and expect you to exit at some point.

But you may have other options up your sleeve that mean escape will be easier. If you took the electrical plans from the Meeting Room table then goto **055**.

If not, where did you park your sidecar?

In the barn – **254**

Hidden in the trees in the orchard – **274**

059

You point your torch into the air and make the flashing signal that declares an abort. There will be no confirmation from the aeroplane and you run back into the ditch, watching the sky as best you can. The aeroplane appears to circle round before flying off to the south. Looking up, you cannot see a parachute and believe the message was understood. You now need to route to the next rendezvous point but as you are about to move out, you can see torches along the route you would take.

Quickly you move away from them but this is taking you further away from the new rendezvous point. You are also holding a line that is upwind of the dogs. To get to the new meeting point you will need to cross the line and route through the torches. The new arrival will not wait at the rendezvous point for long. If you don't meet the arrival then they will try for another meet later tomorrow in town but that becomes trickier and brings a lot of risks with it. Do you,

Take a chance and route through the dogs and torches - **199**

Stay clear of the dogs and torches and risk the meet tomorrow - **179**

060

You keep your head at a tilt hiding behind your hair and tell him you are here for basic help. He seems a little unsure of this and what to do. Calling over to his colleague on the switch board, he asks her to come and see you. She turns around from her switchboard and looks you up and down. Then she tells the soldier she doesn't know you and hasn't seen you in the auxiliaries' quarters. When you turn back to him to plead your case, he has a gun pointing at you and the woman is calling the guard room. Soon you are taken away with a hood over your head and placed into a van. You are driven to a nearby prison. After three months of questions and torture you are led to a wall in a field one day with a firing squad. Here your adventure ends, another hero lost on a foreign field.

You have failed. Maybe you need more than a pair of fluttering eyelashes. Goto 001 to try again.

061

You abandon the dinghy, fearing that it may already have been seen. But now you will have to act quickly as you are stuck in the sea, a sea that is choppy and you are a good distance from the shore. Knowing you can't simply wait for the Germans to disappear, you reason there are two options. You can swim to another part of the beach away from the rendezvous point. These areas were considered dangerous by Headquarters and they would certainly be a risk. But then the safe area has also become a risk. Or you could swim towards the cliffs where you would have to get onto the craggy rocks that meet the sea in this choppy water. They certainly didn't teach you how to do that back at headquarters and it would seem like certain death without some sort of protection. What will you do?

Swim towards the cliffs and hope for the best – **081**

Swim towards the beach and take your chances on this dangerous area -**121**

062

The handle makes a small clicking noise and you see the rope vibrate slightly. But there's no other noise or any problems from upstairs. After this anti-climax, you wonder if you could bring the tray down from upstairs but without knowing if anyone is upstairs, you think this might be foolish. It will probably only be dirty plates at best.

Turning around to the rest of the kitchen you ponder what to do next. If you have not done so already, do you,

Search the cupboards – **002**

Check out the storeroom – **082**

Exit the kitchen – **200**

063

You simply stare forward hoping that he thinks you don't understand. He stares at you directly and repeats his question in English. He looks threatening and pulls out a gun pointing it at your head. Again he asks the question. Do you,

Answer in English – **083**

Keep on looking forward – **103**

Try desperately to apologise in French – **123**

064

There are pictures along the wall which speak of German soldiers, officers and parades. As you walk cautiously up the corridor, you hear laughter coming from a room on the left and also some typing from a room on the right. You are thinking about which to try and explore first when a German soldier steps out of one of the rooms and sees you.

"What are you doing here?" he demands in French.

Do you,

Try and flirt with him, apologising that you are lost – **084**

Say you are new and that you are lost – **104**

Try to overpower him – **124**

065

Oh yes, you say in German, many times. The guard looks at you strangely and then pulls out his pistol. He says it is strange that having been here many times you don't know the standard arrival protocols. He calls another guard and you are searched. Seeing your double uniform, they take you off to the cells of the chateau.

The next day you are questioned and then taken away to a prison where you spend three months in the company of the Gestapo, being tortured for information. You give up some of the details of your former location but it doesn't matter as those things have changed. Then one morning you are taken out into bright sunshine and given a blindfold. Standing at an unremarkable wall, you are shot by firing squad, your mission is over.

You have failed. Following the local intelligence is pretty important. Goto 001 to try again.

066

You remember the bathroom window led to an intermediate roof and would be ideal for using the sheets. This way you would avoid the guard and any of the other household staff. This is certainly a worthwhile option but there may be others. Return to **006** and see if you have any other options before deciding.

067

The Gestapo officer looks at you and shakes his head. "I am not so sure about you. It is like you simply learned things from a book, maybe. We shall see." You are hauled off the train into the arms of awaiting Gestapo soldiers. Later at a prison under intense torture you break down and are seen for the spy you are. At least you don't know anything to pass on before you are executed.

You failed. Best not rely on luck next time. If you want to try again goto 001.

068

You grab the shovel and take a look at it. It is French made and fairly standard in size. It might make a good weapon if needed but you would be very noticeable carrying a shovel. You decide against taking it as it really is not subtle enough for creeping around the barracks.

The boiler suddenly makes a growling sound and you have no idea what that means. The shovel looks recently used and you decide you cannot hang about in case someone comes.

Leaving the boiler room you wonder what to do next. Do you,

If you haven't already, enter the room marked "Store" – **148**

Retreat back to the stairs and climb them – **144**

Retreat back to the front corridor if you have not been that way before – **064**

Or do you think you have something which can get you access to the Cells – **164**

069

You tell the beggar he is now safe and that he needs to stay casual but come with you. The beggar laughs and you see a gun being pulled from within his garb. There's a sickening feeling in your stomach and you try to run. Half expecting a bullet to be your next friend, you instead fall into the arms of the German soldier. You are placed into a van and sent to the local prison, the HQ of the Germans in the area.

There follows days of torture and questions before one day you are awoken early in the morning and taken before a firing squad. All the time you curse yourself for falling for a German trap.

You have failed. You really need to be more careful. You can try again at 001.

070

You see the gate ahead and you think you may even see a resistance car in the distance. Freedom for your prisoner is close and it spurs you on. But then a soldier at the gate spots you in the general melee and fires. You collapse in a crumpled heap and all your worries are over.

You have failed. It was a pretty risky escape plan. Try again at 001.

071

You open the cabinet above the wash basin and see a simple razor and other shaving accoutrements. In the corner of the cabinet you spy something that may be useful. Maybe the General had a lady friend visiting but there is a hair clip in the corner and you pocket it. Some doors with simple locks can be opened with it. You then look around the wash basin but find nothing. (*Deduct 2 mins for this search*)

Return to **011** and choose another option

Or has time gone for you, in which case – **376**

072

Under the table you remove the plans and place them inside your jacket. Leaving the case visible on the table, you go into the ladies toilets and spy a small window above the cistern. Opening the window, you climb onto the toilet seat and pull yourself up and place your legs through the window. You let yourself fall to the ground and land heavily, dirtying your skirt and jacket.

You pick yourself up and walk quickly away from the bar down a small alleyway. Without looking back, you walk fast, listening for anyone following. But there is nothing. After five minutes of being clear of any tail you make your way to the bridge on the other side of town where you can meet your contact.

Goto **271**

073

The globe is impressive, made from wood and engraved with incredible detail. It spins perfectly and must be an expensive item. You notice a catch at the mid-point of the globe and on opening it, you are able to lift off the top half of the item and reveal an interior that is holding a number of decanters and glasses. This is clearly the Commandant's main drink's cabinet. Stylish and sophisticated it is also a complete waste of your time.

It has taken you 2 minutes to examine the globe, but if you have the British airman with you that time has been only 1 minute.

Goto **275**

074

You try your keys but nothing seems to work in any of the drawers. (*You spend 3 mins trying all the keys.*)

Do you have other keys or a hairpin to try – **456**

Or has time gone for you, in which case – **376**

If not return to **416** and choose another option

075

Dressed in your outrider's outfit you ponder the correct response. Do you,

Tell her as she is a mere auxiliary, you want to know what she's doing out here at night – **095**

Run away – **115**

Say you are here looking for a lovely lady like herself – **135**

Do you have chloroform – **155**

076

You look amongst an assortment of tins that are stacked on the larder shelves. There are even some packets of flour and an array of herbs on one shelf. Various cutting boards are also stacked near the bottom of the larder but one thing you note is the small tin which has a tobacco motif on the side. This seems a strange thing to be kept in a larder so you open the tin and find inside a number of pieces of paper. Most are tallies of goods received and used. But one particular piece of paper interests you. It has instructions for how to break a code. You pocket the paper and replace the tin lid with the other papers.

You feel you have spent long enough in this place, especially with a knocked out chef on the floor. Quickly you exit the kitchen. Do you,

Do you enter the Guard room – **096**

Try your luck at the Commandant's Office – **235**

077

If you have already opened this door – **131**, otherwise

You look at the door of the small communications room and it has one lock. The door also seems to be fairly weak and you may be able to barge it open. Do you,

Barge the door open – **097**

Use a key in the lock – **252**

Do you have a hair clip – **197**

Go downstairs and ask the guard to open it for you – **137**

Or do you forget about this door and instead,

Look around the landing for any help – **439**

Try the door that says "General's Office" – **479**

Try the door that says "Communications Room – **216**

Try the unmarked door – **356**

078

You make your way from the hallway to the front entrance where the same two Germans are still there. The soldier behind the desk says hello and nods whilst the female telephone operator turns around and looks at you.

Are you wearing your shoes? If not – **015**

If you are – **035**

079

You decide that the torches and dogs are far enough away to allow the plan to work. You flash the clear-to-jump signal to the aeroplane and the four of you point your torches to the sky to show the drop zone for the parachutist.

You see them jump from the aeroplane but realise the dogs are coming closer. You hold on, shining up into the dark as the aeroplane departs and the night becomes filled with only the noise of dogs and running feet. As you see the parachutist hit the ground, you hear gunfire and fall to the ground in agony. There wasn't enough time but then all your worries are over now. You have become another casualty of war.

You failed. Knowing when to continue and when to abort are key for a spy. Try again at 001.

080

You tell him that you have been requested by the General to complete some work but obviously you cannot discuss that sort of thing. He nods approvingly and takes your hand ushering you down the entrance hall before letting you go when he points out the stairs to the upper floor. You thank him and continue on your way.

Goto **379**

081

You swim hard towards the cliffs, leaving behind the searchlights on the beach. There is seemingly no one on the cliffs and you find yourself hopeful that once ashore you can make your way to a safe point. But in front of you the water is swirling and you find yourself fighting hard just to stay afloat.

More and more, you are not guiding yourself but are taken along by the sea currents and are heading straight into the rocks. You hope that you might get lucky and be thrown ashore, up and clear of the rocks. But the sea is a cruel mistress and you are dragged down and then smashed into the black, barnacle covered mainstays of the cliffs that you cannot even see.

You don't suffer as everything goes black immediately. In the days that follow an unknown body is found on the beach. After being searched and having no documents on it, it is buried in a shallow grave far from the shores of its home.

You failed. Try again by returning to 001

082

You enter the storeroom and are immediately confronted by a chef lying propped up on the floor. He was asleep but your presence seems to have awoken him. He seems quite bleary and looks up at you. Are you wearing,

A German auxiliary uniform - **102**

A German outrider's jacket and trousers - **347**

083

As you shake, you reply in English, "No, I have always lived here." There's a tremor in your voice and the Gestapo officer smiles. "It is often easy to falsify your accent when there is no pressure but you have spoken like an English native. And I think you are. Take her, and the rest of them."

One of your party runs and is shot. The rest of you raise your hands and a van soon arrives to take you away. Soon you are in the same prison as the prisoner you were trying to rescue is in. But unlike them, you don't get a train ride to Germany. Instead, you meet a firing squad on a crisp clear morning a few months later.

You have failed. And in a rather daft way to. Still try again at 001.

084

You smile at the man and tilt your head at an angle before him. Your eyes take on an apologetic look and you reach out to him in hope. You tell him you are lost and that you only want to get back to your job. But also that you are glad that it is him who has found you because you have seen him around and you actually hoped you might meet, alone.

He seems somewhat taken by you and approaches putting an arm around you and even tussling your hair at one point as he directs you back down the corridor.

He says that he will look out for you but at the moment he is a busy man as the Commander has a special guest upstairs.

You retreat back down the corridor until he returns to the room he came from. Obviously the front of the building is too dangerous to look around and you are faced with either going upstairs or to the rear of the building. Do you,

Go upstairs – **144**

Head to the rear of the building via the other corridor – **044**

085

You tell him you have never been here before and he seems satisfied. He tells you that in future, do not make eye contact and simply take out your papers. They will be examined and you can then pass. You apologise and thank him. He says sidecars should be taken up to the barn to the west of the main house and takes your papers for examination. A minute later he hands them back and waves you on, his colleague opening the gates that front the property.

Goto **264**

086

The sheets are a good idea but you don't know of any windows with access to a roof point. There are not enough sheets to manage a drop to the ground from the upper floor. Nice idea but not feasible. You may not select using the sheets. Return to **006** and see if you have any other options.

087

You think you can avoid a papers check if you go to the toilets and you head off in that direction after making your excuses. As you approach them, you hear the Gestapo behind you and you know you need to do something. You could hide in the toilets as surely they wouldn't search the ladies toilets. Or you could get off the train and stand just off it until it starts again. Or you could continue to the guard carriage and hide in the luggage. But you need to make your mind up now. Do you,

Hide in the luggage in the guard carriage - **266**

Hide in the ladies toilets - **246**

Jump off the train and hang around the platform - **226**

088

You take the German uniform down and find it to be nearly dry. It is on the large side for you and you realise that the arms and legs would be too long and would need to be rolled up. However it is a German uniform and may be a better disguise than the maid's outfit. It seems to be of an officer as well so it would give credence to your being in the main house. This could be a lucky break. Or it could look like a pantomime. Do you,

Take the German uniform with you – **108**

Ignore the uniform and hang it back up – **128**

089

You decide to leave the conversation there, thinking this might be a trap. As you stand up you see him flash a glance at the German soldier. There is a tell-tale look and you can see the two men are in cahoots. You really should stay clear of the soldier and this beggar. A good piece of intuition. If you haven't already,

Engage the old woman - **358**

Visit the peasant man - **418**

090

You see the gate ahead and you think you may even see a resistance car in the distance. Freedom for your prisoner is close and it spurs you on. But then a soldier at the gate spots you in the general melee and fires. You collapse in a crumpled heap and all your worries are over.

You have failed. It was a pretty risky escape plan. Try again at 001.

091

The small black case on the floor has an array of bottles inside and a number of cloths. You try to read the labels in the dark and a small bottle of chloroform interests you. Pocketing it and a cloth with which to administer it, you hunt for anything further but find nothing else. Still, you now have a way to disable someone if you can sneak up on them. (*Deduct 2 mins for this search*)

Return to **011** and choose another option

Or has time gone for you, in which case – **376**

092

You decide to hang tight and wait to see what happens. After ten minutes a car pulls up outside the bar and the same German officer who had checked your papers at the train appears and marches up to your table with other soldiers. There are no questions, just hands that take you away.

You are taken to a prison where you are questioned and tortured for three weeks. Then one day you are taken out in the early morning sunshine with a firing squad. In the glorious early dawn you become another fallen hero on a foreign field.

You have failed. Inaction is rarely good. Try again at 001.

093

You look under the lounge and then investigate the recesses of the chair. Turning it over you find it is in fact of Austrian manufacture and over one hundred years old. This has been a nice history lesson that has cost you 2 minutes of your time. If you have the British airman with you it only cost 1 minute.

Goto **275**

094

You take a look inside the wardrobe and find empty hangers there. There are a pair of boots much larger than your feet in the base of the fixture but otherwise nothing else. It appears this is a temporary storage facility used by the General during the day of necessary. (*You have spent 2 mins looking at this item.*)

Return back to **416** and choose another option

Or has time gone for you, in which case – **376**

095

You roundly scold the woman for speaking to you like this and ask what she is doing out here. She seems embarrassed and you perceive she might be meeting someone. You tell her if she minds her own business you will mind yours and not report her. She seems relieved and you walk off leaving her to her secret rendezvous. Is your sidecar,

In the barn – **254**

Hidden in the trees in the orchard – **274**

096

Sneaking up to the guard room you can hear nothing else inside, and so enter gently, glancing around the room. There are a number of lockers, all shut with padlocks. The room itself is immaculate and only a pair of boots are on the floor. On the wall is a notice board with various pieces of typed paper on them. There is also a small window which you can look through if you stand on the wooden benches that sit in the room. You know you won't have long in here and any time spent looking around is increasing the risk. However there may be something of interest or of usefulness in here. Can you afford the time to look? Do you,

Take a look at the lockers - **116**

Get a bench to climb on and look out the window - **196**

Examine the notice board - **215**

Or if you haven't already been there,

Goto the Kitchen - **237**

Goto the Commandant's office - **235**

097

You put your shoulder to the door and hit it hard. It makes a reasonable bang and although the door is forced off its lock you are unsure if anyone heard. For a while you wait and see if anyone is coming. Only when you realise it is quiet do you continue. (*This takes 5 mins to be sure you are in the clear, deduct that from your time.*)

Now enter the room - **131**

Or has time gone for you, in which case - **376**

098

He walks out of the door and you breathe a sigh of relief. Stepping quietly to the door you make sure he has gone before deciding on your next course of action. You daren't stay here as you haven't a lot of time. Do you,

Leave and instead look at the room marked "Boiler" – **028**

Retreat back to the stairs and climb them – **144**

Retreat back to the front corridor if you have not been that way before – **064**

Or do you think you have something which can get you access to the cells - **164**

099

You tell Marcel that you need to cause a diversion to route the dogs and the approaching lights away from here. He looks around him before suggesting that a few of the resistance could intercept the lights and put up a brief fight before running away, allowing you time to get the new arrival and take him away from the area. You suggest that maybe you could go in their place and cause a tactical diversion by pretending to be a lost woman in the night who has fled some men who were dragging her away. You wonder if these options are the best you have. Then you see a small building close by but still at a sensible distance. Maybe you could set that on fire and draw the oncoming dogs and people to it. You look at Marcel for advice but he seems to be looking right back at you. Will you,

Run to the house and set it on fire to cause a diversion – **119**

Tell the resistance to intercept the oncoming lights and engage them for a short time – **139**

Approach the lights yourself pretending to be a lost woman who has escaped some cruel men – **159**

100

You tell the soldier that you have been requested by the General and need to go to his offices immediately. You can see he looks a little dubious and says that it seems unusual for the General to be working at this hour and asks when he called. Do you,

Say it was pre-arranged last night – **120**

Tell him the General called barely ten minutes ago – **140**

101

Rowing towards the other end of the beach, you can see there are large metal barricades and fences along it. High above there are concrete boxes with guns pointing out, searching for any invaders. You fight the dinghy as you reach the breakers and are run into the beach. As soon as the water is shallow enough you leap from the boat and make your way to the first barricade where you crouch down behind it.

Goto **281**

102

The chef smiles at you and you can see him admiring your figure. He stands up and asks you in German what you are looking for in the kitchen. He seems non-aggressive and almost helpful if a little forward. Do you,

Say you were hungry and ask for an apple – **122**

Ask for a rolling pin to do some baking back at your rooms – **142**

Apologise and say you are on your way to the General's room – **162**

103

You continue to look straight ahead, shaking a little but not speaking at all. The German officer laughs out loud and then walks round to your side of the cart. He calls his colleagues in the car, announcing to them that you are a fool. He slaps you about the face before going back to his car, still laughing. The Gestapo drive off and you breathe a sigh of relief. You may have a cheek that stings but you are alive and able to continue the mission. Without further ado, your driver starts the horse moving again.

Goto **183**

104

You apologise profusely and say that you are new here. He swears at you, calling you an imbecile and calls out to another German. He tells you that Helmut hires all the staff and that you will report to him. Briefly, he re-enters the room he came from but then comes out complaining that Helmut is not around and that you may go. He asks your name, to which you say Giselle. He tells you to get back to work, and points down the corridor. Apparently Helmut will speak with you later.

You retreat back along the corridor and know you need to look in another part of the building. Once you are sure he has gone back to one of the rooms, you think about your next move. Do you,

Go upstairs – **144**

Head to the rear of the building via the other corridor – **044**

105

You tell him you have been here once before and he asks why you are here. You hand him your papers and he scans them before handing them back. He tells you that they seem in order but they don't say why you are here. Do you,

Tell him you are here to see the General and as you are an officer of rank he should take notice – **125**

Tell him you are not permitted to divulge that information, you are under orders from the Gestapo – **145**

106

You have the chloroform and cloth and could sneak up on the guard at the stairs and subdue him rather than try to walk past him. This could lead to less complications, such as not being searched. Certainly it is a plan to consider but you may have others to choose from. Return to **006** and see your other options.

107

The German Captain looks at you as you passionately beg his help to escape France. He seems to be warming to your plight until you mention you are a Jew and that is why you need to flee. Without hesitation, he grabs you and takes you out of the cabin and hands you over to the Gestapo, telling them you are Jewish refugee and that he wants rid of you. You are bundled off the train and then into a large van that takes you to prison. Under interrogation they discover your real purpose as a spy and you are sentenced to be shot.

You have failed. Compassion is not often found in war. To try again goto 001.

108

The uniform is too large for you and you would look ridiculous but it may come in useful. You secret it under you skirts and decide to look further around the room.

The boiler suddenly makes a growling sound and you have no idea what that means. The shovel looks recently used and you decide you cannot hang about in case someone comes.

Leaving the boiler room you wonder what to do next. Do you,

If you haven't already, enter the room marked "Store" – **148**

Retreat back to the stairs and climb them – **144**

Retreat back to the front corridor if you have not been that way before – **064**

Or do you think you have something which can get you access to the Cells – **164**

109

Casually you walk past the horse and cart and then look surprised to see the man at the reins. He says hello to you in French and you simply wave back. He asks if you are heading home and you nod, pointing at the old woman with you. Soon you are both up on the cart and the old woman hunches over looking very weary. The horse makes an easy pace and the cart rocks gently as you move along. You control the nerves you feel by clasping your hands together and pray that you can get out of town cleanly.

As you reach the edge of town a small patrol of Germans is inspecting everyone who is travelling beyond the town limits. You sit in the queue and wonder if your new arrival will have the correct paperwork for the soldiers. Your colleague can sense it too and you see his look asking if you need to make a run for it.

Do you,

Nod in reply – **129**

Shake your head in the negative – **149**

110

You see the gate ahead and you think you may even see a resistance car in the distance. Freedom for your prisoner is close and it spurs you on. But then a soldier at the gate spots you in the general melee and fires. You collapse in a crumpled heap and all your worries are over.

You have failed. It was a pretty risky escape plan. Try again at 001.

111

The uniform on the back of the door is neatly pressed and looks ready for wear. You begin to carefully search the pockets and inner lining. As you make your way through the jacket's inner lining you find a discrete pocket, small and tucked away with a faint opening. Inside is a key with a yellow label. You take this and continue your search but you can find nothing else. (*Deduct 2 mins for this search*)

Return to **011** and choose another option

Or has time gone for you, in which case – **376**

112

You tell the officer that you are staying with friends and he nods. He asks you which friends and why they have not met you here. You say that you have been before and did not want to give them any trouble. So he offers to take you to their house. You try to say it's fine but two soldiers take you to the officer's car. When he asks for the address, you say you don't know and that you only know the route, he says you must take them there.

You carry on the charade until you pick a house. The officer takes you to the front door and when the couple that answer look at you bemusedly, the officer takes you in for questioning and confiscates your case.

You are taken to a prison where you are questioned and tortured for three weeks. Then one day you are taken out in the early morning sunshine with a firing squad. In the glorious early dawn you become another fallen hero on a foreign field.

You have failed. Stories you can't back up are never a good idea. Try again at 001.

113

The filing cabinet is unlocked and you have to wade through a large number of files detailing the operations of the barracks and the daily records of provision supply and personnel movements. However a section labelled Commandant's office grabs your attention and inside one of the files you find a coded message which states that these are numbers for the door lock. The message is just a lot of letters. Who knows how to break it?

It looks like this:

DGDRFRCCL JCDR

RUCLRWQGV PGEFR

CJCTCL PGEFR

The search has taken you 2 minutes, or only one if the British airman is with you. Cross that time off now. If you try to break the code, you must time how long you are spending doing that, and remove that time from your remaining time until the Commandant comes back.

Go back now to the decision page about searching the room. You can stay there while you work on the code if you wish but remember to deduct time spent on the code. Having the British airman with you does not half the time you work on the code as only you are working on it.

If you have a code book **-133**

Otherwise goto **275**

114

Opening the door of the drinks cabinet, you find inside a number of bottles of schnapps and even a bourbon, secured from some American no doubt. There are tumblers and brandy glasses, all of the finest cut crystal. But there isn't anything useful. (*You have spent 2 mins searching here.*)

Return back to **416** and choose another option

Or has time gone for you, in which case **- 376**

115

You run away from her and she begins to shout. Soon there are cries all over the place and you see shadows running everywhere. Only the power not coming on saves you from searchlights and the bright glare of lamps in the chateau grounds. But the Germans have organised and are soon hunting you with dogs and torches.

Trapped within the chateau grounds, you manage to evade capture for an hour before a dog appears and grabs your leg, holding you until others arrive. You are lead to a van where a black cloth is placed over your head. You wake up in a cell and from there you suffer three months of questioning and torture. Then on a sunny, crisp morning you are led away to a small wall, accompanied by six soldiers and an officer. There you are shot by firing squad, another hero who falls on a foreign shore.

You have failed. Running is rarely the answer. Try again at 001.

116

You look at the first locker and find it padlocked. Pulling down on the padlock, it is firmly secured and you wonder how to break it open without making a lot of noise. There's certainly no way to force it without making a racquet.

Do you have the vials from the store – **136**

Do you have a lock pick – **156**

Or is the best you've got your own plucky determination and know how – **176**

117

Congratulations, the door clicks open and you have a way out of the room. Goto **312**

118

You grab the soldier from behind and he elbows you in the midriff. Grabbing your hand, he tells you to know your place, telling you to be grateful that you have a job with the great German army. Again he slaps you across the face, before walking away. Do you,

Let him leave – **138**

Attack him again -**158**

119

Racing away from your colleagues, you reach the small house and find it to be an empty ruin with a large amount of vegetation growing in it. Being summer, most of the vegetation is dry and there are numerous old dead branches and items, including some wood. You quickly take some matches from your pockets and begin to start a fire. It seems slow at first but then it catches, causing you to run from the building lest you get burnt. Soon the whole building is ablaze, small as it is, and you race into the darkness satisfied that your work has been done well.

From a distance you watch the lights and the dogs begin to make for the building. You can only hope that this has been enough and that the new arrival is safely with your colleagues. Keeping an eye on the Germans who have arrived into the light of the roaring fire, you make your way to the rendezvous point for the next part of the operation.

Goto **218**

120

You tell the soldier it was arranged last night and he nods approvingly. Explaining that all the calls would come through that switchboard and there hasn't been any for over three hours, he thought it strange that you would have been in contact with the General. But as it was last night, he is satisfied. He points down the entrance hall towards a large staircase much further down before getting back to his work on the desk. Do you,

Walk on through the entrance hall – **379**

Talk to the switchboard operator – **180**

121

Swimming towards the beach, you can see there are large metal barricades and fences along it when your head gets to bob above the waves. High above these defences are concrete boxes with guns pointing out, searching for any invaders. You fight the breakers and eventually stumble your way onto the beach, clothes sodden. You realise you need cover and quickly make your way to the first barricade where you crouch down behind it.

Goto **281**

122

You smile broadly at him and say you were just a little hungry and were looking for an apple. Laughing gently, he says that you know that the food from this kitchen is only for the General and other special guests in the chateau. However, since you look lovely he will sneak you an apple just this once. He turns and hands you one from the shelf behind him. Thanking him you turn away and you know he is watching you as you leave. With this in mind you have to take the exit to the hallway. As you do he says, with a yawn, that if anyone asks where that apple came from, it wasn't here. You say thank you and leave through the exit to the hallway.

Goto **200**

123

You start to babble in French, apologising, asking why this is being done to you, and saying that you've had no trouble so far. As you reach a crescendo, the officer walks around to you and places the gun right at your head and then says "Shush!"

You stop talking and your body shakes as you wonder if he is going to kill you. He starts laughing before lowering the gun and holding you by the chin and placing a kiss on your lips. He turns to his compatriots and laughs again, making a sign with his hand that the air is smelling as you have defecated.

You breathe a sigh of relief beneath but your outer expression is one of fear and you keep it as the Gestapo car pulls away. It may have been an embarrassing and scary situation but it has worked out well and you don't hesitate in telling the driver to move on and get to the house.

Goto **183**

124

You try to grab him with both hands but he is strong and holds you by the wrists. By the time you aim a kick at his groin, he is already calling out to the other Germans in the nearby rooms. Soon you are overwhelmed by a number of them and are taken to the barracks commander.

They find out that you do not work here and you are placed before a firing squad along with some maids who are suspected with bringing you into the compound. Your war is over.

You have failed. Maybe try and be more subtle in life. But at least you can begin again at 001.

125

He disappears inside and you can see him on the telephone. You are sweating when he comes back out and tells you to go on ahead but take a left at your first opportunity. You watch the gates being pulled apart and then speed through looking for the first left to park the sidecar. But as you turn several Germans step out with machine guns. There is nothing to do but surrender. They take you off to the cells of the chateau.

The next day you are questioned and then taken away to a prison where you spend three months in the company of the Gestapo, being tortured for information. You give up some of the details of your former location but it doesn't matter as those things have changed. Then one morning you are taken out into bright sunshine and given a blindfold. Standing at an unremarkable wall, you are shot by firing squad, your mission is over.

You have failed. A senior officer riding a sidecar? Goto 001 to try again.

126

Time to select a plan. Remember you can only choose those which you have the equipment for and the knowledge of:

Do you simply walk down the stairs and out of the door – **146**

Do you get the sheets in the ottoman and then escape via the bathroom window – **345**

Do you sneak up on the guard using the chloroform you hold – **365**

Do you look to place the plans in the dumb waiter and lower them downstairs before collecting them later – **480**

127

You ask the German Captain if you can have a moment and he tells the junior Gestapo officer to wait outside the cabin briefly. The Captain is looking anxiously for an explanation, which considering what he has just done is justified. You need to tell him a better story or look for another way to get his help. Do you,

Tell him you are an escaping Jew and need his protection, saying you will offer him anything in return **- 107**

Offer the Captain money to assist you, saying that as an American reporter you are not too sure the Gestapo will want you around **- 147**

128

You decide it's too much of a risk and hang the uniform back up.

The boiler suddenly makes a growling sound and you have no idea what that means. The shovel looks recently used and you decide you cannot hang about in case someone comes.

Leaving the boiler room you wonder what to do next. Do you,

If you haven't already, enter the room marked "Store" – **148**

Retreat back to the stairs and climb them – **144**

Retreat back to the front corridor if you have not been that way before – **064**

Or do you think you have something which can get you access to the Cells – **164**

Retreat back to the front corridor if you have not been that way before – **064**

129

Your message is understood and the driver of the wagon yanks on the reins and the horse bolts forward. You hang onto the seat as the cart bounces about. Without hesitation the Germans pull their guns and you see the old woman beside you get hit in the chest and tumble off the cart. Next your driver is shot and you pick up the reins. Shouting at the horse to go faster, you break the German line and race with all you've got to the outskirts.

Behind you, the sound of motorcycles fills the air and you know that you will soon be caught if you don't do something. You can see a wood up ahead on your right, or there's the corn fields to your left. Or you can just hope for the best and race on along the road. Do you,

Continue on the road – **169**

Make for the woods – **189**

Make for the corn field – **208**

130

With the gate in sight you hold onto your escapee and run as hard as you can. There is a general melee happening and soldiers seem to be confused as to where they should be. The low manning on the gate is making life easier for you as well. You race through the gate and run out onto a small road where you head for the nearest ditch. Within a minute you hear the approach of a car and panic that the Germans are on to you. But then the face of a French woman heartens you and her resistance friends pull you into a car and you speed off. Your head is kept down but it is only a few minutes before they tell you that you are clear. You made it with your prisoner!

Goto **150**

131

Inside the "meeting room" you see a large table around which there are eight chairs. On the table are a selection of plans and a number of left over cups. In the corner is a dumb waiter, presumably going down to a kitchen. Around the room are pictures on the wall of the Führer and of various monuments to German greatness. A bank of telephones sit on a table at the far wall and there is a large window with curtains drawn across it opposite the door. A small plant sits on the floor at the corner of the room. (*This quick look has cost you 1 min but only if this is your first time at 131*) Do you,

Look at the dumb waiter – **151**

Examine the plans on the table – **171**

Check out the pictures on the wall – **191**

Take a look at the telephone bank – **210**

Have a peek out of the window – **250**

Or does the plant take your fancy – **270**

If nothing here is of interest then return to the landing and

Look around the landing for any help – **439**

Try the door that says "General's Office" – **479**

Try the door that says "Communications Room – **216**

Try the unmarked door – **356**

Or has time gone for you, in which case – **376**

132

He seems fascinated by your travel plans and asks which train you are taking out and can he see your ticket. Your eyes scan the departure boards desperately and you see a train for Paris. You tell him you haven't purchased the ticket yet but that you intend to right now. The officer follows you and watches you purchase the ticket. You have two hours until that train leaves and you sit down in the train station. The officer continues to watch you.

You need to get moving to meet your contact but you have the watchful eyes of this German on you. Do you,

Go to the ladies toilets and try to escape from there – **152**

Board a train leaving the station and jump from it shortly after leaving – **172**

Cause a scene with the officer and claim he is harassing you to the station staff – **251**

133

You cross reference the label on the code with the code book and find the cipher. Every time a letter is used it is replaced by the letter two after it in the alphabet. Handily, there's a decryption chart.

Code in **Bold**, Translation in *Italic*

A B C D E F G H I J K L M N O P Q R S T U V

Y Z A B C D E F G H I J K L M N O P Q R S T

W X Y Z

U V W X

Goto **275**

134

You peer carefully out from behind the blackout curtain looking down to the compound. There are very few lights on and you can only see the odd cigarette end in the distance at the perimeter. You know you will have to escape from this place but you were hoping to drive out calmly, or sneak over the wall. Staring as hard as you can, you can't determine anything more about the compound than you already know and so decide to get back to what you should be doing. (*You have wasted 2 mins staring out the window.*)

Return back to **416** and choose another option

Or has time gone for you, in which case – **376**

135

You tell her you are on the lookout for a lovely woman like herself and she seems to be creeped out. But she takes your hand and leads you away from the shed and towards the front of the chateau. But as soon as she sees a guard she calls out and says she has an intruder. You break off and run for your life.

However your life is not that much longer as a guard targets you in his sights and brings you down. After that there is nothing, as you become another hero lying on the soil of a foreign land.

You have failed. It's not a Hollywood film where the chat up lines always work. Try again at 001.

136

You take one of the vials and pour the contents onto the padlock and watch as the acid burns through the retaining bar. With ease you slip off the lock through the gap created and open the locker. There's some photographs and a lump of cheese. There's also a note at the bottom of the locker which has three numbers written on it. 15 left, 26 right, 11 right. *Copy this nnto the Notes section.*

You wonder if it's important and stash the note on your clothing. Quickly searching the rest of the locker, you find nothing important and shut the door again.

Time is precious and you decide you have lingered long enough here. You go to the door and plan your next move. Do you, if you haven't already,

Go to the Kitchen – **237**

Go to the Commandant's office – **235**

137

You go downstairs and ask the guard to come up and help you enter the room. When he gets to the top of the stairs and realises that you are trying to gain access to the meeting room, he points his gun at you and asks you to accompany him downstairs. He says no one has access to that room except the senior staff and certain auxiliary staff who all have their own signed for keys.

You have no reason to be there and he suspects you are a spy. He takes you at gunpoint to the front of the building where he finds additional guards.

You are covered with a hood and find yourself next in a cell. For days you are questioned and tortured, giving up many secrets. After three months you are led away to a wall in a garden where you are shot by firing squad. Your last memory is the sound of birds chirping their morning calls, then rudely interrupted by the crack of gunfire.

You have failed. You actually asked the enemy for help? Goto 001 to try again.

138

You watch him go cursing him under your breath. But you know any further attack could expose you. You nearly let the mission go for a sense of offended pride. Waiting at the door, you make sure the corridor is clear before stepping out. Do you,

Leave and look at the room marked "Boiler" – **028**

Retreat back to the stairs and climb them – **144**

Retreat back to the front corridor if you have not been that way before – **064**

Or do you think you have something which can get you access to the Cells – **164**

139

You tell Marcel to take most of the men and make a diversion by intercepting the lights. He looks a little anxious about this but he grabs two men and runs off into the night. You start to signal the aeroplane indicating the drop zone but you have worries. The pilot will only see two torches not four.

Suddenly you hear shooting nearby and realise that Marcel and his friends are in a battle with the Germans. The aeroplane can also hear the gunfire as it abruptly sets off to the alternative drop zone. Your instinct is to follow it and meet the parachutist there but you see that although Marcel has engaged some of the lights, another set are moving round into your path, blocking your access to the second drop zone. You have to move away and go to the rendezvous point for the end of the operation. You cannot see if Marcel or any of his friends have made it clear but there was a lot of shooting. Deep down you feel anxious and panicked for their safety.

Goto **258**

140

You tell him the General called only ten minutes ago to request you. The soldier looks concerned and you see him pull his pistol and point it at you. He shouts over to the switchboard operator, asking if there have been any calls in the last few hours. Turning on her seat to face you both, she says no and then looks closely at you. She says she doesn't recognise you from the auxiliaries.

You turn to the soldier to plead your innocence but he has a gun pointed at you and the woman is calling the guard room. Soon you are taken away with a hood over your head and placed into a van. You are driven to a nearby prison. After three months of questions and torture you are led to a wall in a field one day with a firing squad. Here your adventure ends, another hero lost on a foreign field.

You have failed. Ooh, that lie backfired. Goto 001 to try again.

141

Dipping your oars into the water, you pull away from the lights, taking yourself back out and giving yourself time to think about what to do next. If there are Germans at the rendezvous point then maybe the contact would have gone elsewhere, or maybe they have just run. Either way you need to get ashore as if you are out in a dinghy in daylight that will attract patrols from the Germans and capture.

Looking along the coast you realise there are two main choices. You could head for another part of the beach. This would give a safe landing but you know from Headquarters that certain parts of the beach are not secure and you have been warned that landing there would not be advisable. On the other hand, you could make for the cliffs and try to land ashore there. But the water is choppy and that could be difficult. Whatever happens, you know you cannot stay here for long and that you need to be ashore and clear of the area by daylight. Time to get moving.

Do you row towards the cliffs? - **161**

Do you row for the other part of the beach – **101**

142

You realise you could do with this chef being out of the way in case he raises an alert so you ask him for a rolling pin so that you can do some baking back at the rooms where you stay. He grins at you and then turns to the shelf behind him and lifts off a rolling pin. He hands it to you and you start to swing it in order to bludgeon him on the head. But as you pull back he holds in his free hand a pistol pointed at you.

He marches you at gunpoint to the front entrance where several guards take you into custody. As you are put into handcuffs they are asking him how he knew you were a spy and he says that you asked to make food in your room which is strictly forbidden on this site. How could you have known?

You are take away in a van to a nearby prison. After three months of questions and torture you are led to a wall in a field one day with a firing squad. Here your adventure ends, another hero lost on a foreign field.

You have failed. Things made up on the spot sometimes back fire. Goto 001.

143

As you shake you reply in English, "No, I have always lived here." There's a tremor in your voice and the Gestapo officer smiles. "It is often easy to falsify your accent when there is no pressure but you have spoken like an English native. And I think you are. Take her, and the rest of them."

One of your party runs and is shot. The rest of you raise your hands and a van soon arrives to take you away. Soon you are in the same prison as the prisoner you were trying to rescue is in. But unlike them, you don't get a train ride to Germany. Instead, you meet a firing squad on a crisp clear morning a few months later.

You have failed. And in a rather daft way to. Still try again at 001.

144

You creep up the staircase trying to keep as quiet as possible and listen out for any signs of conversation or movement. As you reach the landing, you can see three doors leading off it. The one behind the stairs has the word "Kitchen" on it in German. Toward the front of the building are two rooms, one saying "Guard Room" and the other "Commandant".

You can hear voices coming from the Commandant's room, at times loud and angry but always in German. The sound of chopping is coming from the kitchen but you cannot hear any noise from the guard room. Where will you go?

Goto the Kitchen - **237**

Goto the Guard Room - **096**

Goto the Commandant's office - **235**

145

You tell him you are just a delivery man and you are under orders from the Gestapo. He gulps, nods his head and then signals to his colleague. The gates open up and he tells you that sidecars are normally parked up at the barn beside the main house. You nod and ride through the gates.

Goto **264**

146

You place the plans inside your uniform and make your way to the stairs where you can see the guard looking the other way. Calmly you descend the stairs, almost nonchalant in your manner and give a large yawn as you reach the last step. The guard turns and tells you to halt. He says it's standard protocol that everyone who has been up in the General's quarters has to be searched.

Do you ask for a female to search you – **166**

Do you make a run for it – **245**

Do you tell the guard that you have been with the General and that he's not going to take kindly to having his favourite auxiliary searched – **265**

147

How impoverished does this German Captain look? Do you think he has money? Has he debts to be paid back home? Does he just want more money, or like you enough to help? Let's find out.

Try **167**

Or try here **187**

148

You enter the storeroom and are amazed how large it is. In one corner you see a large basket of washing left by someone. On one wall is a cabinet, rusting but apparently unlocked. There are also a number of bicycle tyres on the wall as well as a garden hoe. Amidst the rubbish in the other corner you see some jerry canisters. The room seems to be a dumping ground and there are many odds and ends lying around which don't seem to be of any use.

You may not have long here so what will you look at to aid your mission, or is this all just junk to avoid? Time is precious so you may not get to see everything. Do you,

Look at the bicycle tyres on the wall – **168**

Check out the garden hoe – **188**

Examine the jerry cans – **207**

Look at the rusted cabinet – **227**

Examine the washing basket – **247**

Leave and instead look at the room marked "Boiler" – **028**

Retreat back to the stairs and climb them – **144**

Retreat back to the front corridor if you have not been that way before – **064**

Or do you think you have something which can get you access to the Cells – **164**

149

You shake your head, relying instead on the preparedness of your colleague sat beside you. The old woman never seems to panic but inside clutches at her back, showing the pain she is in. When the German soldier comes up to her and asks for her papers, she swears loudly before reaching into her clothing and producing an identity card. After scanning it intently, the soldier gives it back before moving on to your own papers. Again he gives nothing away but hands them back before checking the driver too.

With a single wave you are dismissed and the driver picks up the reins and you trot forward out of town. It takes a good hour to wander the distance home but you are simply relieved to have gotten out of town. Before long you arrive at the farmhouse and are ready to deliver your passenger.

Goto – **053**

150

You have made it and back at the farmhouse base that night you tell London in code of the success of the mission. You have a great feeling of satisfaction at the success you have enjoyed but you know that you will be called on again soon enough. Find out your next mission at **005**.

151

The dumb waiter is in the up position and you can see the tray that moves up and down is currently on your floor. On it sits a number of dirty plates and you deduce that this must have been a long meeting as the plates have not gone downstairs yet. You pick at a little bit of meat that remains, your taste buds crying out in hunger at the late hour. You could lower the dumb waiter down but to what end? (*You have spent 1 min looking at this object*)

Return to **131** and choose another option

Or has time gone for you, in which case - **376**

152

You go into the ladies toilets, out of sight of the officer, and enter a small bathroom. You spy a small window above the cistern of the toilet. Opening the window, you climb onto the toilet seat and pull yourself up and place your legs through the window. You let yourself fall to the ground and land heavily, dirtying your skirt and jacket.

You pick yourself up and walk quickly away from the station down a small alleyway. Without looking back, you walk fast, listening for anyone following. But there is nothing. After five minutes of being clear of any tail you make your way to the bridge on the other side of town where you can meet your contact.

Goto **271**

153

You take a look out of the windows, taking care to keep below the eye line of others looking up. You can see a concentration of Germans towards the East side of the barracks whilst the West side looks fairly sparse. There's also a laundry van parked by the front door. You also take a look around the curtains and find that they are thick and heavy, presumably excellent in the winter months.

Your search has taken you 2 minutes.

Goto - **275**

154

That's correct. Well done. Now use Number C, Number D and left or right from the middle of your code to generate another page number and go there. If it makes no sense then go to **292**. Goto your next page now.

155

You pretend to be hurt and bend over while the auxiliary comes close. But under that cover you are tipping some chloroform onto the cloth you carry. As she reaches you, you grab her and place the cloth over her mouth. She soon drops, out cold, and you drag her behind the shed where she cannot be seen. After watching the next guard go past, you make for your sidecar. Is it,

In the barn – **254**

Hidden in the trees in the orchard – **274**

156

You take the lock pick out you found in the kitchen. This seems like a simple lock and it is, the mechanism springs open within a minute of manipulation. Removing the lock you stare inside the locker.

There's some photographs and a lump of cheese. There's also a note at the bottom of the locker which has three numbers written on it. 15 left, 26 right, 11 right. *Write this code in the notes section at the back of the book!*

You wonder if it's important and stash the note on your clothing. Quickly searching the rest of the locker, you find nothing important and shut the door again.

Time is precious and you decide you have lingered long enough here. You go to the door and plan your next move. Do you,

Goto the Kitchen – **237**

Goto the Commandant's office – **235**

157

You try different keys from the loop of keys you obtained in the kitchen. The door opens after the fourth try and you step cautiously inside. (*Take 1 min off your time*).

Goto **131**

Or has time gone for you, in which case – **376**

158

You make another grab at him but he is half expecting it and turns round catching you before you can hit him. Grabbing your wrist he drags you kicking and screaming to the front of the building where he shouts at a junior officer to dispose of you. The officer says he doesn't recognise you as one of the wash women.

The original officer calls you an imposter who is in a secure area. There is no trial but instead you are taken outside the barrack grounds by a group of soldiers where you are shot by firing squad. Your days as a spy in this war are done.

You have failed. Anger is the undoing of so many people. Try again at 001.

159

Taking off your black top to reveal farm clothes underneath, you head towards the lights and dogs. There's a crashing through the undergrowth as you get closer and you are felled by the leap of a black dog which proceeds to sit on top of you growling. Its wet jowls drip onto you and you wonder if it will attack. But it is called off by a German soldier and you are lifted to your feet by two men.

They frog march you to an officer who starts to bombard you with questions in French about why you are here. You tell of how you were dragged away by some men who intended for you to be with them that night except that you escaped. You are a frightened young woman, looking to get home. The officer continues to probe you with questions until a soldier returns to him and tells him in German that a parachute was seen coming down.

He speaks no further to you but instead orders for you to be taken away to the local prison where you occupy a cell for three months. Each day consists of torture and questions. But the punishment is soon over as you are led away and shot one cold morning. You never know if your sacrifice was the price paid for a successful mission.

You may or may not have failed but it was a short war for you. Try again at 001.

160

You tell the soldier that you have work upstairs, for the General, and you need to get it done before morning. He seems puzzled and you say that it is unusual but the General will be wanting it in the morning so you need to get it done now. This seems to satisfy him and he points the way down the entrance hall, letting you go. Do you,

Walk on through the entrance hall - **379**

Talk to the switchboard operator - **180**

161

The water is cold as you leap from the vessel. You hope they haven't heard the splash and swim away quickly from the dinghy, praying it will either not be found or will be a distraction allowing you more time to get away.

The water is bouncing you about and you cannot simply remain out here, or you will fatigue and drown. But where do you make for now? The target point is obviously compromised but you could still take your chances on the other parts of the beach. It's risky but there are not many options. The other idea would be to head for the rocks but getting out of the water onto the rocks would be nigh impossible in such rough water. What do you do?

Route towards the cliffs - **081**

Swim towards the other part of the beach - **121**

162

You tell him you are on your way to the General's rooms and thought you heard a noise. He looks at you suspiciously, asking why you are on your way there at this time of night. Do you,

Tell him it's for a secret mission that you can't talk about - **182**

Tell him you don't question orders and it's none of his business - **327**

163

You start to babble in French, apologising, asking why this is being done to you, and saying that you've had no trouble so far. As you reach a crescendo, the officer walks around to you and places the gun right at your head and then says "Shush!"

You stop talking and your body shakes as you wonder if he is going to kill you. He starts laughing before lowering the gun and holding you by the chin and placing a kiss on your lips. He turns to his compatriots and laughs again, making a sign with his hand that the air is smelling as you have defecated.

You are relieved underneath but your outer expression is one of fear and you keep it as the Gestapo car pulls away. It may have been an embarrassing and scary situation but it has worked out well and you don't hesitate in telling the driver to move on and get to the house.

Goto **183**

164

You stand before the door to the cells which is locked. How will you break it open?

Do you have a key – **184**

Do you have a number of small vials – **203**

Do you have something else – **223**

165

You pull up at the gates and take your papers out for inspection. When the guard arrives you hand them over without comment and he checks them for the next minute. He then waves you on and tells his colleague to open the gates. As the large fixtures are being opened, the guard says that sidecars are parked up in the barn next to the main house. You nod and then ride through the open gates.

Goto **264**

166

You tell the guard that is of course fine but you would like to be searched by a female if that was okay by him. He looks at you suspiciously but then decides that your request is not unreasonable. He shouts down the corridor to the front entrance for the radio operator but there's no response. Telling you to wait he walks down the corridor. Do you,

Simply wait – **186**

Hide the plans in a nearby plant pot – **205**

Run – **487**

167

There seems to be a smugness coming over his face and you realise you have reached a soft spot. You agree an amount and he steps outside of the cabin. Within minutes the Gestapo leave and you are sat inside the cabin as the train continues on its way. But you now have a German captain to deal with.

When the train reaches the next country stop, you ask him if he will take a quick stroll with you for air. He agrees and you both alight from the train disappearing behind the small station. You spy a bottle on the ground and secret it on your person. As you allow him a kiss, you crack the bottle off his head, knocking him out. Quickly you board the train, knowing you'll be off elsewhere by the time he wakes up.

Goto **206**

168

You take a bicycle tyre off the wall and it looks pretty much as expected. As you spin it round in your hands you see a note fall out of it. It is in German and details that the West gate is depleted by four with one remaining today. There is no other writing on it except today's date. You wonder what it could mean but then you hear someone entering the room.

The sound of boots fill your ears and you gulp hard as you are about to be discovered.

Goto **232**

169

You shake the reins as hard as you can but a motorcyclist pulls up beside you brandishing a gun. He indicates you should pull over but you instead swing the horse towards him and he is hit by the cart before he can get a shot off. Unfortunately you didn't spot the other motorcyclist arriving on the opposite side and picks you off with a clean shot to the head. You never even feel the crash of the cart.

You have failed. Not the greatest escape attempt ever made. Try again at 001.

170

You remember looking out of the windows and seeing the laundry van sitting outside. It seemed deserted and it's also right outside the door. You could sneak your prisoner down into the van and then drive off quickly hoping to get through one of the gates.

Have you been in the store – **190**

If not – **329**

171

You pick up the various plans on the table and immediately a set jump out at you. They are electrical diagrams which seem to show the wiring throughout the chateau. With these to hand you might be able to take out the power to the buildings, searchlights and other devices which would be useful during your escape. The other plans don't have any reference points which you recognise and are therefore useless. You pocket the electrical plans and move to the next object of interest. (*You have spent 3 mins looking at the plans*)

Return to **131** and choose another option

Or has time gone for you, in which case – **376**

172

You see a train is ready to depart and then watch it begin to move. Reaching into your case you break out the plans and place them in your jacket. You can see the Germans moving towards you and kick off your heels. You run at the train, grabbing the door of a carriage and pulling it open. There's a gunshot that pings off the train and you fling yourself into the compartment. Inside is a nun and she merely sits there while you clamber in.

The train rumbles out of the station and you leave the door hanging open. After a minute it is passing close to the river and you make a leap from the train in the dark. You have no way of knowing what is below you. Let's hope you are lucky.

Choose **192, 211** or **231**

173

You take hold of his bonds and untie him. He seems somewhat wobbly and you are not sure just how coherent he is. You ask him in English if he knows of anything in the room which can help and he points towards the Commandant's desk. But beyond that there is little forthcoming.

This act has taken you 2 minutes, or only 1 if you have the British airman with you.

Goto **275**

174

You decide the code to set for the tumble locks and spin the two digit code on the first dial, then on the second and then on the third and try the handle, your heart in your mouth.

To see if you are successful, take the first digit of each two digit code you enter and place them in order first, second and third. This is the entry you should now go to. If the entry makes no sense the safe doesn't open and you should return to **029**. (*Note each attempt takes up 1 min of your time.*)

Or has time gone for you, in which case – **376**

175

Dressed in your auxiliary outfit you are the woman's equal and need to come up with a good excuse. Do you,

Tell her you are awaiting a German soldier on a secret rendezvous – **195**

Tell her you are merely enjoying the night air – **214**

Do you have the chloroform – **234**

176

Well you check out the lock, thinking about how you could break it open. But you haven't got anything with which to effect any influence on the lock. After spending a few minutes on the problem you realise you cannot just sit around here and you need to get moving. Leaving the room you wonder where to go next. Do you,

Goto the Kitchen – **237**

Goto the Commandant's office – **235**

177

You try your keys but alas none fit. You try and jiggle them about but to no avail. (*After 2 mins you stop, realising these keys are not correct.*)

Go back to **077** and choose another option.

Or has time gone for you, in which case – **376**

178

You throw yourself at the man clawing at him with your hands. You gouge him across the face but he swings an arm that connects with you and you tumble backwards, tripping up and cracking your head on the floor. When you awaken, you find yourself tied to a chair with a German officer asking you questions.

Soon you are moved to a prison where you spend three months being interrogated. Then one morning, instead of the interview room, they take you outside with a small squad of soldiers. You are shot by firing squad, one more hero who never sees her homeland again.

You have failed. Raw power doesn't work if they have more than you. Try again at 001.

179

You indicate to Marcel that you need to stay well clear of the dogs and torches and he leads the team in a direction opposite to the one you would like to follow. You walk a few miles before you are taken into a barn where the team stop to discuss what to do. The parachutist will have hopefully made it to the second drop zone and will have then headed off into the dark to find tomorrow's rendezvous point. There is nothing further to do now except disband, get some sleep and then try again tomorrow.

Goto **278**

180

You walk over to the switchboard operator and ask her about where the women are able to go in the chateau. She looks at you and seems to be pondering. Without replying to you she shouts across to the desk soldier and tells him she doesn't know you, you haven't been in quarters and you certainly haven't been about the office.

You turn to the soldier to plead your innocence but he has a gun pointed at you and the woman is calling the guard room. Soon you are taken away with a hood over your head and placed into a van. You are driven to a nearby prison. After three months of questions and torture you are led to a wall in a field one day with a firing squad. Here your adventure ends, another hero lost on a foreign field.

You have failed. Let sleeping dogs lie. Goto 001 to try again.

181

You row hard towards the rocks and the sea becomes choppier, throwing the dinghy this way and that. You feel glad you have the vessel because you reckon you couldn't swim in that sea. As the rocks come closer you hear the dinghy clatter onto them and you decide you'll have to make a jump for it onto the best rocks available. You try to steer close to one of the smoothest and largest rocks but the dinghy hits something underneath and you make a leap of faith.

Fortunately your feet find something solid and you scramble across slippery but fairly flat rocks, making your way to the base of the cliffs. You see the dinghy continue to be thrown about and so decide to move away quickly. The path is not that clear but you focus and pick your way along. However with your head down you fail to see a man step out in front of you.

He's wearing a cloth cap, black jacket, grey trousers and black shoes. With a gun pointed at you, you gulp wondering if he is going to fire. But maybe he's your contact. They have said nothing about what he looks like only where you would meet him. But he would have seen the activity on the beach, surely? Maybe this is worth a risk, maybe you need to take a chance. Then again, your luck might just run out. Do you?

Speak the code word given to you by Headquarters for meeting your contact – **201**

Blag a story in French about how you have been abandoned by your boyfriend – **221**

Wait for him to speak- **241**

182

He tells you to wait a moment and leaves the storeroom to enter the hallway beyond the kitchen. You get a bad feeling and think you should leave, but as you are about to go, he returns with a guard who he says will take you to the General since you are clearly lost.

You are taken upstairs to the General's rooms but you never see him. The guard checks out your story and you are found out as a spy and taken to a van outside where you are covered with a hood. You are taken away to a nearby prison. After three months of questions and torture you are led to a wall in a field one day with a firing squad. Here your adventure ends, another hero lost on a foreign field.

You have failed. Things made up on the spot sometimes back fire. Goto 001.

183

You enter the house which has curtains drawn and all lights extinguished. There is a supply of explosive in the side room and you spend twenty minutes going through it and making sure you have detonators and the correct connections. With everything checked and ready, you gather your team in the dark and are joined by a resistance runner.

He says that the station is well guarded whilst the track by the woods has only minimal guarding. However the bridge seems to be well secured and will require a painstaking approach, upstream and then a silent climb through the metal under the bridge. This will take time.

You think about this as the runner goes on to talk about Gestapo cars. It seems that there will be several available for taking and then using to follow the prisoner's car back to wherever they take him next. It is unlikely he would simply return to the prison.

You need to make choices about your plans for tonight. First, where will you plant your bombs?

Will it be the train station – **242**

Will it be the remote track near the woods – **262**

Or will it be the bridge – **382**

184

You take out the key you found in the boiler room and try it in the lock. The door opens with a clunk and you go inside.

Goto **243**

185

You pull up in front of the gates and simply wait there for someone to come. A guard comes out and asks what you want. He seems unhelpful and quite direct with this statement as if you have done something wrong. Do you,

Apologise but say you have a message for the General – **204**

Tell him to open the gates as you have a message from the Gestapo – **224**

Tell him you have been assigned here – **244**

186

You wait until the guard returns with a woman from the front desk. She eyes you suspiciously and begins to frisk you. It isn't long before she feels the plans in your jacket and pulls them out to show to the guard. He takes you out of the chateau and holds you at gunpoint until a van arrives. The plans are taken from you and you are covered with a black hood.

You wake up in a cell and from there you suffer three months of questioning and torture. Then on a sunny, crisp morning you are led away to a small wall, accompanied by six soldiers and an officer. There you are shot by firing squad, another hero who falls on a foreign shore.

You have failed. Sometimes you have to do something. Try again at 001.

187

As you begin to mention money in return for his help, he becomes indignant and says he would never betray his country for a mere sum of money. He flings open the door and tells the Gestapo officer of your attempt to bribe him. You are whisked off the train and placed into a van with a blindfold on your head. When you next see light, you are in a prison cell and a man is asking you questions. The next few weeks are difficult as you are tortured for information. You never see England again, another casualty of war lost in a foreign field.

You failed. If you want to try again then goto 001.

188

Taking the garden hoe down from the wall, you examine it and find it to be a little bit rusty. The handle is wooden and rotting a bit but the iron at the end seems to be solid enough. Maybe this could be used as a weapon. It's not easy to conceal however.

Just then you hear someone coming, the clip of German boots on the concrete floor outside. The bile rises up in your throat as you realise you are about to be discovered.

Goto **232**

189

You turn the cart towards the woods and race off into the trees. You hear the motorcycles come to a halt and men shouting behind you. This will be a matter of luck rather than any skill in these woods. You hear the shots coming behind you but does a bullet have your name on it. Let's see.

Goto **228**, **248** or **268** and see how lucky you are.

190

You remember the washing basket in the store and decide this would be a great disguise for the prisoner. You could wrap him in sheets and pretend he's carrying them as he gets into the back of the van.

Do you have the British airman with you – **209**

If not but you want to try this plan - **329**

If you don't like this plan - **312**

191

You walk up to the first picture on the wall of the Führer and examine behind it, lifting it away from the wall. There seems to be nothing extraordinary about the painting or indeed the frame and you quickly move onto the next picture. One by one you give each of the images a thorough going over but they seem to be simply pictures and frames. (*You have wasted 3 mins checking out the pictures*)

Return to **131** and choose another option

Or has time gone for you, in which case – **376**

192

You land awkwardly and tumble down a slope. As you fall you hit your head off a rock and everything goes to black. And that's all you know as you die from your fall.

You have failed. It was a risky jump. Try again at 001.

193

You approach the lock and see the dial where you will have to enter the code to open the lock. The dial is set to zero and you will have to spin it left or right to different numbers. If you don't know the code or don't want to try to open the door at this time then return to **275.** You will need to deduct 1 minute of your time for looking at the mechanism.

If you want to try use the codes you have to open the door then use the following formula to go to your next page:

The code you have will be in the form (number A, number B, *left or right*/number C, number D, *left or right*/number E, number F, *left or right*). Take the first part, (number A, number B, *left or right*). Goto the page that has the numbers (number A, number B, left or right). If the answer is left that becomes the number 4, if the answer is right, that becomes the number 7.

Example if your code was 56 right, 34 left, 98 right you would initially go to page 567, that number A =5, number B = 6 and right = 7

Work out the page you need to go to now. If the entry makes no sense you have the wrong code and you should go to **292.** Goto the page you code gives now!

194

You dial in the last of the dials and pray as you turn the handle. It twists and you pull open the door. Inside you see a file with a red binding, entitled Operation Snow Hammer in German. This is what you have been looking for and you place it inside your jacket. There's a palpable sense of relief that at least you can now go but you need to work out the best route of escape from the chateau. After that it will be a trek to England. Start your escape at **006**

195

You tell her rather sheepishly that you are awaiting a German soldier who promised you a walk under the stars. The woman seems embarrassed saying she is here for the same thing. You generously offer to keep her secret if she keeps yours and tell her you will move off to intercept your man a little further away. She nods in a show of feminine solidarity and you walk away. But where is your sidecar?

In the barn – **254**

Hidden in the trees in the orchard – **274**

196

You grab a bench and drag it to the window. Standing on your tip toes you can just about see out of the window and notice that there is a significant number of guards marching to their posts. Most seem to be heading east though and not so many out to the western perimeter. You wonder if this is important but your eye is caught by a laundry van sitting just outside the building. There seems to be little activity around it.

You think you can hear movement downstairs and this reminds you that you cannot simply hang about in this guard room. You decide you need to move on and find the prisoner and so you go to the door of the room. Do you,

Goto the Kitchen – **237**

Goto the Commandant's office – **235**

197

You take the hair clip from the bathroom and try it on the lock. It takes a bit of fiddling but the door opens. (*It takes you 2 mins, so deduct this from your time.*)

Enter the room now at **131**

Or has time gone for you, in which case – **376**

198

You grab the garden hoe off the wall with one hand and swing the implement into his face. He stumbles backwards and you then hit him with the handle over the head. He tumbles to the ground and you jump on top of him. But there's no need as he is out cold.

Using some of the tyres you tie up his hands and gag him. It's very rough and ready but hopefully you won't be here much longer. You decide to leave the room as if anyone else comes you won't be able to explain the bound German officer. Do you,

Leave and instead look at the room marked "Boiler" – **028**

Retreat back to the stairs and climb them – **144**

Retreat back to the front corridor if you have not been that way before – **064**

Or do you think you have something which can get you access to the Cells – **164**

199

You indicate to Marcel that you all need to move through the German ranks and meet the new arrival. He seems worried but goes with your judgement. You creep forward and think you may have found a gap when a dog barks out loud. Another joins it and you realise they have your scent. Immediately you start to run but you are pursued and there are lights now shining in your direction.

When the gunfire starts you manage to run behind some trees but you notice that the rest of the mission team don't manage to follow you, probably shot. When you clear the trees you hear gunfire and your legs give way. Your last memory is a dog sniffing at your face and a torch shining bright.

You have failed. You ran right into the enemy and crossed the upwind line. Brave but foolish. Try again by going to 001

200

You are in the hallway beyond the kitchen and are aware from local intelligence that the General functions out of offices and accommodation upstairs in the chateau. You know that there is a main staircase towards the front of the house that will take you to the area of the chateau you need to be in and so you walk slowly down the hallway towards the front of the building. Arriving at a door, you gently open it and see a guard with his back to you at the foot of the stairs. He seems quite tired as you can hear him yawning gently.

The guard stands at the bottom of a wooden staircase that has an ornate carpet beginning from the floor but running up the stairs. At least your journey up will be quiet. The rest of the space at the foot of the stairs is lit by a few lamps but is rather gloomy.

You will need to get past this guard if you are to have access to the rooms above but it is the middle of the night and you will need a good excuse. You haven't got anything around you that would help, so you desperately search the space around the staircase with your eyes. What story will you come up with? Do you,

Take your papers out and hold them as you pass the guard, pretending they are documents for the General – **219**

Tell the guard that the General requires you for some urgent typing – **299**

Tell the guard that you need access to the documents upstairs – **319**

201

The man stares at you when you say the words "Jesu adore les petite enfants." Then he lowers his gun and indicates that you should follow him. The climb up the cliffs is difficult but your guide seems to know where he is going and at the top, just as dawn is breaking, you are placed into a hay cart, driven by another man. Under the hay is some cheese and a flask of water which you try to consume as you bounce along. The journey is hot and long and you wonder how many miles you have travelled before a woman pulls back the hay.

You struggle to move your body, locked up from having been stuck in the one position for so long. You are taken into a hay barn and shown the top floor where you spend the rest of the day. Occasionally someone brings food and water but no one stays for long. The people looking after you say very little, and it's only when a tall dark man arrives in the late evening that you find someone who speaks instead of indicating.

"Good evening Mademoiselle, you have done well, I am glad to see you survived. Shall we talk about the next part of your journey?"

Goto 401

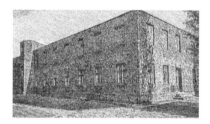

202

Let's go, you cry, and the horse is driven onward at speed, kicking up the dust on the road. The car watches you pick up speed and then follows you. You pass by the rendezvous house, not daring to stop and then try to cut down a side road. The cart is going too fast and it overturns throwing you all to the ground. You hear the car arriving behind you and have no time to see if anyone else is okay. Instead you bolt away and hope the others follow you.

From a nearby field you see the Gestapo officer radio in instructions as he stands over the body of one of the brave resistance fighters. While you watch you are joined by some of the other fighters who were in the back of the cart. Together you decide to continue the mission and route quickly and off road to the house where you will pick up the explosives. But there are German soldiers everywhere now, alerted by your escapade. There is no way of getting through to the house and no way of reaching the explosives.

You have failed. Your over reaction has caused the abandonment of the plan and of the prisoner. This will greatly affect the war. Still, maybe try again at 001 and not be so hasty next time.

203

You take one of the vials you found in the cupboard and wonder just how strong the acid is. Carefully, so as not to get it on your hands, you crack the vial above the locking mechanism. The liquid runs onto the catch and starts to dissolve it. Part of you is in disbelief at the strength of the acid but another part is starting to feel a little awkward about carrying the remaining vials.

The acid gives off a pungent smell but soon you see the catch has dissolved and you open the door with ease. Quietly, you step inside.

Goto **243**

204

You quickly apologise for the sudden arrival but say you have a message for the general. The guard tells you that because you haven't followed correct procedures he will have to search you. There's no choice and you step off the sidecar motorcycle and allow him to search you. He finds the gathering of your skirt and doesn't see it as a chubby belly. His search intensifies and he removes your hat, finding your hair tied up beneath. You have been rumbled. There is nothing to do but surrender. They take you off to the cells of the chateau.

The next day you are questioned and then taken away to a prison where you spend three months in the company of the Gestapo, being tortured for information. You give up some of the details of your former location but it doesn't matter as those things have changed. Then one morning you are taken out into bright sunshine and given a blindfold. Standing at an unremarkable wall, you are shot by firing squad, your mission is over.

You have failed. Not following the enemy protocol can hurt. Goto 001 to try again.

205

You quickly take the plans and place them in a nearby plant pot. By the time the guard returns you are standing in the same spot and are ready to be frisked. He has brought a female auxiliary and she eyes you suspiciously. But despite a thorough search she finds nothing and starts to walk back towards the front desk. The guard tells you are free to go and quickly runs after the woman, possibly looking to get a date with her.

You take the moment and retrieve the plans from the plant pot, slipping them back inside your jacket. Now you need to get to your transport. Did you come in via the kitchen or the front entrance? Best to route back the way you came as you know what's there. Did you,

Come in via the kitchen - **058**

Come in via the front entrance - **078**

206

The train journey continues and you see fields pass by wondering when you will be off this train and onto the next stage of your mission. At a small outlying station, a woman in a smart coat and high heels gets onto the train and sits in your cabin. She speaks to you politely in broken English, saying she is a French aristocrat, hoping to meet her husband, a man high up in the Vichy government. She suggests you could interview her when you tell her you are a reporter. When you say you are from New York, she says she is from Philadelphia and your heart skips a beat. Two stops later, you both leave the train.

Goto **482**

207

There are some six jerry cans of what smells like petrol. It seems to be a strange place to keep fuel and you are not sure how long they have been there. You think about carrying one but there are heavy to lift and too clumsy to sneak about a building with. Looks like they are not of any use just now.

Just then you hear someone coming, the clip of German boots on the concrete floor outside. The bile rises up in your throat as you realise you are about to be discovered.

Goto **232**

208

You jump off the cart and run into the cornfield stumbling as you go. You hear the motorcycles come to a halt behind you and a shot races through the corn stalks beside you. The stalks are far from fully grown and you may need to get lower but this will slow you down. You need to decide now what your best chance is. Do you,

Keep running at full height – **288**

Get low down and crawl – **308**

209

Your friend suggests that you could place the prisoner into the basket and then both of you carry him to the laundry van. This sounds like a great way to avoid the Germans.

If the British airman is in a German uniform – **229**

If not, but you knocked out a German in the store – **249**

If neither of these apply then you point out the flaw in your friend's plan being that he doesn't have a disguise. Instead you'll need to cover them both in sheets that they carry and hope for the best as you run to the laundry van.

If you like this plan – **349**

If not then go back and chose another one – **312**

210

There are a total of 6 telephones in the bank and all sit silent at this time. They are on a cabinet with wheels, allowing the furniture to be moved closer to the main table. The first in the series is red but the other telephones are all a grey colour with no particular markings on them. There's no dust on the telephones and you can see they are well used. (*This analysis has taken up 1* min) Do you,

Leave the telephones and examine something else. If so, goto **131** and choose another option.

Pick up the red telephone and see who is at the other end – **230**

Or has time gone for you, in which case – **376**

211

You tumble into the black and your feet go from under you. Your leg clatters into a rock as you fall and you think it might be fractured or broken. It hurts like crazy but you know you need to keep moving or you will be captured. Hauling yourself to your feet you spy the bridge where you will meet your contact and move out in that direction.

Goto **271**

212

You sit beside him and he offers you some drink. He rambles on about all sorts of nonsense, complaining about how the weather is not as good as it used to be, how wine is declining and also how pretty girls look these days. You sit in silence beside him but he never questions why you don't speak. This is getting you nowhere. Do you,

Talk out loud to the beggar – **049**

Leave the beggar and if you haven't already,

Talk to the old woman – **358**

Talk to the peasant man – **418**

Talk to the German soldier - **298**

213

Carefully you tiptoe into the room and can see a bed at one end. Some covers lie over a man who is snoring lightly. There are several items of furniture in the room including a wardrobe, a dressing table with several items on it and a small ottoman, an upholstered seat with no back or head. There is also another door opposite from the entrance. Although well co-ordinated and reasonably lavish, the room is nonetheless small and you will never be more than a few feet from the sleeper if you search it. As the windows are blacked out by curtains, you will need to get close to the objects in the room to make a proper assessment of them. (*You have used up 1 min on this quick look around. This is only deducted on your first time at 213*)

Do you,

Examine the dressing table – **233**

Check out the wardrobe – **393**

Or (see over the page)

Look closely at the sleeper – **433**

Look out of the windows – **473**

Search the ottoman – **340**

Try the door across the room – **011**

Or maybe this is all too risky and you would rather

Look around the landing for any help – **439**

Try the door that says "General's Office" – **479**

Try the door that says "Meeting Room" - **077**

Try the door that says "Communications Room – **216**

Or has time gone for you, in which case – **376**

214

You tell her you are merely out here to enjoy the night air. This makes her anxious and she says that you are not supposed to be here and that you cannot be here. She is becoming emotional and you try to grab her to calm her down. But instead she screams bringing guards towards you. You run but a guard lets off a round which sends everything to black, a sleep you don't wake up from.

You have failed. It was a pretty lame excuse. Try again at 001.

215

The notice board has several pieces of paper pinned to it, all written in German and with a seal on the foot of them. Apart from some general orders, you are most intrigued by the guard rotation that indicates that the West entrance of the compound will not be so heavily guarded today as the East side. This is due to some activity seen on the eastern side. Further perusal of the papers reveals nothing else of note.

Time is precious and you decide you have lingered long enough here. You go to the door and plan your next move. Do you,

Goto the Kitchen – **237**

Goto the Commandant's office – **235**

216

If you have already opened this door – **290**

Otherwise the door is locked and will need opening. It has a simple key lock. Do you,

Try to force the door - **236**

Go back downstairs and get the guard to open the door – **256**

Do you have keys to try in the locks – **276**

Do you have a hair clip - **336**

Or do you give up on this door at the moment and instead (*but take 1 min off your time if you choose any of these options*) choose one of the following:

Look around the landing for any help – **439**

Try the door that says "General's Office" – **479**

Try the door that says "Meeting Room" - **077**

Try the unmarked door – **356**

Or has time gone for you, in which case – **376**

217

You let the officer drag you along and he takes you to the room at the front of the building where there are a large number of officers. He asks them in German if any have sent you to the storeroom and gets no reply in the affirmative. He then calls for a junior officer and asks him if he recognises you as one of the wash women. He says no and you are taken outside. He calls you an imposter who is in a secure area. There is no trial but instead you are taken outside the barrack grounds by a group of soldiers where you are shot by firing squad. Your days as a spy in this war are done.

You have failed. Sometimes you have to back up your lies so it's better if they are half-truths. Try again at 001.

218

You meet up with your friends from the resistance but they tell you that the aeroplane diverted to the alternative drop zone, maybe because they saw the fire. Unfortunately the resistance couldn't go to the zone because the German line of torches was directly in their path so they have routed back here to assess the next part of the plan.

Goto **238**

219

Pulling together all your courage you walk right up to the guard with your papers in an envelope in your hand. He asks you your business and you tell him that the General has requested the documents in your hand. The guard seems surprised and narrows his eyes as he looks at you. You smile but he still seems unappeased and ask what the documents are. Do you,

Tell him you are only delivering documents and it wasn't your place to ask when you were given them to transport – **239**

Tell him they are just routine troop movement information – **259**

Tell him it is personal family correspondence and that you may be required to bring back his replies – **279**

220

You reach out and try to grab him. He shouts and runs off claiming you are trying to get him to collude and that he wants nothing to do with you. The German soldier comes over and begins to ask questions which escalates the situation. Suddenly you find yourself under suspicion and you see more soldiers approaching. There appears to be no way out and you begin to run. A single shot takes you down and ends your mission in France.

You have failed. Sometimes you need to let people go. Try again at 001.

221

You don't trust this man and begin to tell him in French how you have been abandoned by your husband. He seems appreciative but stills holds a gun at you. Eventually he indicates that you should turn around. As you rotate, you feel a blow to the back of the head. Waking up, you are in a German cell, cold and dank, with a basic bed. You find out you have been captured and are questioned about who you are. The rest of the war is short lived for you and you are just one more spy who never made it back home. But at least you had no secrets to share.

You failed. Goto 001 to start again. Lucky you, real spies don't get that chance.

222

Goto **043**

223

You take out your item and try it on the lock but to no avail. Looks like you haven't got the right piece of equipment. Time to regroup. Do you,

If you haven't already, enter the room marked "Boiler" – **028**

If you haven't already, enter the room marked "Store" – **148**

Retreat back to the stairs and climb them – **144**

Retreat back to the front corridor if you have not been that way before – **064**

224

You tell him to hurry and open the gates as you have a message from the Gestapo. He asks for who and you rally that if he delays you there will be investigations. You can see him panic and he turns to his colleague to open the gates. But he also demands your papers which he gives a cursory glance at when you hand them over. Just as the gates open fully, he waves you on saying that sidecars are parked in the barn adjacent to the main house. You ride through the open gates.

Goto **264**

225

You realise you are in trouble and run out of the door. Unfortunately, a guard is patrolling outside at that moment and hears the cries of the soldier at the entrance desk. You hear a loud crack and then see nothing more.

You have failed. Sometimes you can't just run. Goto 001 to try again.

226

You step casually off the train as if you are getting some fresh air. As you glance about the platform, you realise there are a lot more Gestapo soldiers around than you thought and you try to smile and look about as if there is nothing wrong at all. But from the corner of your eye, you notice a Gestapo officer is staring intently at you. You try to feign a little surprise, as if you would be the last person to be suspected of anything but he is now moving your way. You feel like you need to do something but to run away would be foolishness as you would be caught almost straight away. There is a man standing close to you in a smart suit and smart shoes. He is talking in French to another man. Maybe you could use him as a decoy. Or maybe your papers will be good enough under scrutiny. Do you,

Kiss the Frenchman as if you are meeting an old friend – **286**

Smile at the Gestapo officer as he reaches you - **306**

227

Opening the rusty cabinet, you wince as it squeaks open. Inside there are a number of small vials of a clear liquid. Beside them is a printed piece of German notepaper which has various chemical formulae on it. You try to read it through but some of the language is beyond your capacity, however you do recognise the section that states the liquid is a very strong acid. Maybe that could be useful. You secret a few of the vials in your clothing.

Just then you hear someone coming, the clip of German boots on the concrete floor outside. The bile rises up in your throat as you realise you are about to be discovered.

Goto **232**

228

Goto **268**

229

With the airman in a German uniform and you dressed as a maid, you place the prisoner in the basket in the store and then carry him to the back door. Waiting for a good moment, you walk together to the van getting very few looks from anyone. As you reach the van you open up the rear of it and are delighted to find no one inside. You then make your way to the front seats and find there are no keys in the ignition. The airman reaches underneath and fiddles with the wires and jump starts the van. You pull away slowly and have only one more obstacle to freedom, the gate. Do you go for:

The east gate – **269**

The west gate – **289**

The north gate – **309**

230

You pick up the red telephone and put it to your ear. You hear a click and then a voice identifies herself as the switchboard before waiting for a reply. You put on a gravelly voice and say you are just checking the telephones before putting down the receiver. You turn to look at the other items in the room but in the distance you can hear footsteps. You race out of the meeting room and try to make it down the stairs but you are spotted. A soldier opens fire and you tumble down the steps. You are another brave hero who has fallen in a foreign field.

You have failed. Better to look and not touch. Try again at 001.

231

You tumble into the black and your feet go from under you. Your leg narrowly misses a rock but your hand hits it, possibly fracturing it, or even breaking it. It hurts like crazy but you know you need to keep moving or you will be captured. Hauling yourself to your feet you spy the bridge where you will meet your contact and move out in that direction.

Goto **271**

232

A rather portly German dressed in a smart uniform enters the room and stares hard at you. He looks around the room and then apparently satisfied that there is nothing to fear asks you "What are you doing here?" in French.

Your mind spins, what should you do? He looks unfit but is a lot bigger than you. Do you,

Explain that you have been asked to go here by a German officer – **287**

Grab the wash basket and say you are just sorting the washing – **307**

Attack the man with your hands – **178**

Attack the man with the garden hoe – **198**

233

The dressing table has a small stool underneath it and two small drawers on the side. It is sparsely decorated as befits a man's table and has a small photograph of a child on the left hand side and a note on the right. Otherwise there is little of interest and you wonder what to look at first. (*You have used up 1 min of your time searching.*) Do you,

Read the note – **253**

Search the drawers – **273**

Examine the photograph – **293**

Or do you decide to look elsewhere. If so return to **213** and chose another option

Or has time gone for you, in which case – **376**

234

You pretend to be hurt and bend over while the auxiliary comes close. But under that cover you are tipping some chloroform onto the cloth you carry. As she reaches you, you grab her and place the cloth over her mouth. She soon drops, out cold, and you drag her behind the shed where she cannot be seen. After watching the next guard go past, you make for your sidecar. Is it,

In the barn – **254**

Hidden in the trees in the orchard – **274**

235

You step towards the Commandant's office and hear the door begin to open. Quickly you dive into the guard room and hide behind the door, peeping out to see what is occurring. You see a German officer backing out of the door. He shouts back into the room in English, "I will return in twenty minutes when you shall give me a better answer." With that you watch him stride away and go down the stairs.

The door closes and you go to it and listen. There is only the sound of a man in pain and you decide it's worth the risk to open the door as this could be the prisoner you are looking for.

You open the door and step inside. In front of you is a man tied to a chair. He has obviously been beaten in the last few days and he seems somewhat sullen. But as he recognises you have entered the room, he tells you to stop the door from closing. You spin around but it is already too late.

You ask why the door was so important and he says it is a safety feature of the room that when the door closes it locks from the inside. It requires a code to be opened and used on the dial.

You are trapped. In nineteen minutes the commandant will return and discover you in here and then the game will be up. You need to use this time wisely. Looking around the room for help, you can see the Commandant's desk, a china hutch, a large globe in the corner, a chaise longue and a filing cabinet. There are also windows at the front of the room currently obscured by curtains.

You wonder what to do to start as you have only a fixed amount of time and looking in the wrong place may lead to disaster.

Go to **255**

236

You put your shoulder to the door and hit it hard. It makes a reasonable bang and although the door is forced off its lock you are unsure if anyone heard. For a while you wait and see if anyone is coming. Only when you realise it is quiet do you continue. (*This takes 5 mins to be sure you are in the clear, deduct that from your time.*)

Now enter the room – **290**

Or has time gone for you, in which case – **376**

237

You enter the kitchen and see a man in a white hat chopping carrots at the side with his back to you. He is tall and thin and doesn't seem to notice your arrival. The kitchen itself is fairly small and must be the Commandant's personal one. You can see lots of cupboards and cooking utensils, as well as a sink and a small larder at the rear of the kitchen. Do you,

Speak to the chef in French - **257**

Speak to the chef in German - **337**

Try to overpower the chef - **457**

Leave quietly and try one of the other rooms - **016**

238

Huddled in a barn you await further details from resistance runners. On their return you find that the parachutist did come down in the drop zone and safely made an escape. This means that the new arrival will try and make contact in the town tomorrow near the riverbank as per the fall-back in the plan. There is nothing further to do tonight except get some rest and then prepare for the meeting tomorrow in town. You feel uneasy that this will be done in daylight and right under the noses of the Germans.

Goto **278**

239

You advise him that you are only the messenger and you don't ask what you carry when you take papers to the General. He seems suspicious and asks to see the documents. You breathe in deeply as he takes the envelope and you pray he won't actually take the documents out. Unfortunately for you, he is thorough and pulls out your papers.

He immediately points his gun at you and takes you to the front reception area where a second soldier telephones for other guards. You are taken to a cell in another part of the chateau and are then interrogated in the morning. From there you are taken a week later to a prison. After three months of questions and torture you are led to a wall in a field one day with a firing squad. Here your adventure ends, another hero lost on a foreign field.

You have failed. Things made up on the spot sometimes back fire. Goto 001.

240

You try to hit the door with your shoulder and it causes a loud bang. You hold your breath waiting to see if you have disturbed anyone. You hear some shuffling from downstairs but fortunately no one comes up the stairs. When you are sure it is all clear you think what to do next. (*Take off 5 mins for trying to force the door and then waiting until you are sure no one is coming.*)

Go back to **479** and try another option.

Or has time gone for you, in which case – **376**

241

He remains quiet and looks at you. He is clearly is waiting for your reaction. So do you?

Speak the code word given to you by Headquarters for meeting your contact – **201**

Blag a story in French about how you have been abandoned by your boyfriend – **221**

Wait for him to speak- **261**

242

Planting the explosives at the station will mean that following the car with the prisoner afterwards will be easy. As the train arrives, he will be waiting and you can soon identify in which car he is and follow him to whatever destination they take him to. You tell two of your French resistance colleagues to acquire a Gestapo car just before the train arrives and then to follow the prisoner car.

It all seems so easy as you sit waiting in the shadows of the station. There are lots of Gestapo soldiers around as well as regular German soldiers. In fact it is very claustrophobic and you begin to worry about getting back out of town after the explosion.

Just before the train arrives, you see some agitation amongst the Gestapo officers and then you see your resistance colleagues, the ones who were acquiring a car being brought forward. They are quickly questioned and when they fail to speak they are shot. The Gestapo cars speed off and the train doesn't appear. You can hear it but it must have stayed outside the station, and that's where they will make the transfer. You desperately try to reach this transfer but you are seen by one of the many soldiers and are cut down in a hail of bullets just as another French resistance fighter sets off the bombs and blows up the station.

You have failed. Probably an error in tactics but why not find out by starting again at 001.

243

Behind the door you find a small number of cells, two on either side. There's a chalkboard on the wall which seems to have writing on it. From your current position, you can see that the nearest cell on the left has a French peasant man currently lying down. On the right, you can see a British airman trying to scratch something on the wall. You cannot see the other cells but there are no sounds coming from them.

You haven't got a lot of time so you may need to think about who you want to speak to. Or do you want to simply look around? But shouldn't you try and release these captives too? What will you do? Do you,

Examine the far cells – **263**

Talk to the French Peasant man – **283**

Talk to the British Pilot – **303**

Check the chalkboard on the wall - **488**

244

You tell the guard that you have been assigned here. He asks why you are arriving in the middle of the night and you say you were delayed. However he is not satisfied and asks for your papers. Handing them over, you watch him scan them carefully several times before going to the guard hut and telephoning someone. When he comes back he has a pistol pointed at you.

He tells you there are no transfers today or yesterday and he asks you to step off the motorbike. You have no choice, you have been rumbled. There is nothing to do but surrender. They take you off to the cells of the chateau.

The next day you are questioned and then taken away to a prison where you spend three months in the company of the Gestapo, being tortured for information. You give up some of the details of your former location but it doesn't matter as those things have changed. Then one morning you are taken out into bright sunshine and given a blindfold. Standing at an unremarkable wall, you are shot by firing squad, your mission is over.

You have failed. Not following the enemy protocol can hurt. Goto 001 to try again.

245

You immediately run away but he reacts very quickly. He shouts once and you don't respond. The next thing you know is that you are in pain and falling after a loud bang has split the air. After that you know nothing.

You have failed, shot down in a foreign field. Pity as you were so close. Try again at 001.

246

Looking up and down the corridor of the train, you see the Gestapo officer heading your way. You walk quickly, but not too quickly along the corridor, and then lock yourself into the toilet. You guess you had better make a good show of it and you put the seat down, pull your tights down and then hitch up your skirt. You sit there in silence and listen to the Gestapo moving along the train corridor outside

There's a knock on the door. You freeze and hope they just go away. Then there's another knock, this one louder and firmer. Again you say nothing. But then a third knock comes, louder than any before and a voice tells you to open up the door. Do they know you are in here, or are they guessing? You are trapped so do you just wait and hope they go away or do you open the door? Choose now,

Open the door – **406**

Stay quiet and hope they go away – **446**

247

You grab the washing in the basket and turn it over and over. There are shirts and trousers and all sorts of underwear. Basically, it appears to be the uniform wash for some of the German soldiers which has been dumped here. Maye it's contaminated somehow. As you search through it you see the rust stains on some of the shirts. This is probably a special clean.

Just then you hear someone coming, the clip of German boots on the concrete floor outside. The bile rises up in your throat as you realise you are about to be discovered.

Goto **232**

248

You run this way and that in the woods but then a bullet catches your thigh, this slows you down and although you struggle on, you are hit in the head from close range. There is nothing further as you become another hero lost on foreign shores.

You have failed. Sometimes luck doesn't favour the brave. Try again at 001.

249

You remember the German you knocked out in the store where the wash basket is and reckon the British airman could put on that uniform. You go to the store with the two men and the airman gets dressed.

Goto **229**

250

You take a look out of the window behind the curtains and can see a large part of the chateau grounds. Although it is dark, you can make out the patrol guards pacing across the grass lawns and pathways. You wait, watching, for two minutes but nothing else comes to light. (*Deduct 2mins from your time*)

Return to **131** and choose another option

Or has time gone for you, in which case – **376**

251

You go up to the officer and start shouting at him complaining that he is watching you and following you. Telling everyone you are an American citizen and he has no right to treat you in this way, like you are some sort of threat to him, you demand that the train staff help you.

But they just turn away. After all they are in an occupied country and have little say in what goes on. The Gestapo officer smiles and says that you will be coming with him. Two soldiers take you and your case away to their local headquarters where they strip the case and find the plans.

You are taken to a prison where you are questioned and tortured for three weeks. Then one day you are taken out in the early morning sunshine with a firing squad. In the glorious early dawn you become another fallen hero on a foreign field.

You have failed. After all you've been through, that was your best plan? Try again at 001.

252

Is it a key that you obtained from the kitchen – **157**

Otherwise – **177**

253

The note is in German and speaks of a code necessary to disarm something. Your German fails you as to what is being disarmed but the numbers 14, 25, 97 are highlighted in bold with the word pulley. You don't know what else to make of it and need to move on. (*This examination has taken 2 mins.*)

Return to **233** and look elsewhere.

Or has time gone for you, in which case – **376**

254

You make your way to the barn which is quiet and deserted at this hour of the morning. If you have stashed your outrider's outfit here, you don it again. Finding the sidecar you came in on, you fire it up and are about to drive out of the barn when you hear a terrific hue and cry.

Did you take out the electrics – **314**

If not, there are a large number of lights coming on all around the grounds, soldiers shouting and cries of a thief. You shake a little knowing you still have so far to go to get to the gate. Do you,

Go as quick as you can stopping for no one – **334**

Drive out slowly, gauging what is happening – **354**

255

Make a note of your time in the notes section at the rear of the book. It initially starts at 19 minutes. When you complete an action you will be advised of the time it took to complete that action and you should reduce this remaining time figure accordingly. If you run out of time simply go to the out of time section indicated.

Now be quick, your life and that of those with you depends on it!

Go quickly to **275**

256

You go downstairs and ask the guard to come up and help you enter the room. When he gets to the top of the stairs and realises that you are trying to gain access to the communications room, he asks why you haven't got your own key with you. You tell him you have forgot it and it is at the other end of the compound. You reach out and touch his hand asking if he can help you rather than you walk all the way back. Your feminine touch works and he opens the door for you saying that you should come and get him when finished, so he can lock up.

You thank him, wait, and watch him go back to his post before you enter the room properly. (*This whole palaver takes 5 mins which you should deduct from your time.*)

Enter the room now - **290**

Or has time gone for you, in which case – **376**

257

Do you have the British airman with you? Is he in British uniform – **277,** or German uniform – **297**

Or are you alone – **317**

258

You wait back at the barn, the rendezvous point, for what seems like an age but Marcel and his friends do not return. Your stomach feels sick as you await news from runners sent out to try and discover what has happened.

Your colleagues have been killed and their bodies have been taken to the local prison, the German's temporary base, presumably to be searched and maybe then their photos paraded as a deterrent to further resistance. You step outside and vomit when you hear the news.

But you cannot rest and grieve, for the new arrival has managed to parachute successfully at the second drop zone but they made off into the dark and no one knows where they are now. Following the plan, they should now look to meet at the riverbank in town tomorrow. There is nothing for it but to get some sleep and then plan out what will be a dangerous grab right under the noses of the Germans.

Goto **278**

259

The guard looks at you with narrow eyes and sizes up your story. Standing there awaiting his judgement you try to look natural and calm but inside you are shaking. Eventually he nods at you to continue up the stairs but he says don't be long.

You are about to climb the stairs but at this point mark down in the notes section at the back of the book that you have 30 mins of time to operate before the guard will become suspicious. In the following passages you will be advised when to deduct time and what to do if time runs out.

Good luck and goto **419**

260

You approach the chef from behind but then you stand on a rogue spatula on the floor and he turns to see you with your arms raised in attack. He runs off to a nearby table and you follow. After chasing round and round, he manages to make a bolt for the door and starts shouting on the landing for help. You are trapped upstairs and soon guards fill the floor.

You are captured and taken to a van outside where a hood is placed over your head. After a short journey, you are deposited into a cell and the bag removed. This turns out to be your home for the next three months as you are interrogated. Every day there are questions and pain until one bright morning you are lead to a wall in a field and face a squad of German soldiers. This is where your war ends, another hero lost in a foreign field.

You have failed. Attack is not always the best form of defence. Try again at 001.

261

The standoff continues and he then indicates that you should turn around with his gun. As you rotate, you feel a blow to the back of the head. Waking up, you are in a German cell, cold and dank, with a basic bed. You find out you have been captured and are questioned about who you are. The rest of the war is short lived for you and you are just one more spy who never made it back home. But at least you had no secrets to share.

You failed. Goto 001 to start again. Lucky you, real spies don't get that chance

262

You decide that the best place to plant the explosives is at the remote track thereby blocking the train getting into town. But you'll also need to get someone to steal a Gestapo car for you to use to follow the car with the prisoner when the train exchange doesn't happen. There are bound to be a lot of Gestapo and German soldiers in town and getting the car could be difficult, so maybe you should send the majority of your team there to get the car. The track is weakly defended so you can probably plant the explosives without a large team. On the other hand the primary goal is to stop the train and you may need forces to secure your task if extra Germans turn up. How will you play this one? Do you,

Send most of the team to secure a car in town – **282**

Keep most of the team to plant the explosives – **302**

263

Walking past the nearest cells you take a look at the cells beyond. On the right the cell is empty and doesn't look like it has had any recent habitation. But the cell on the left has a blanket and looks like the bed was used recently. You can also smell urine in the bowl provided for the purpose. However there is no one here. There's not a lot more to learn here. Do you,

Talk to the French Peasant man – **283**

Talk to the British Pilot – **303**

Check the chalkboard on the wall - **488**

264

As you ride up the long and sweeping driveway towards the main house, you see three roads stemming off this main drive. To the west of the chateau is a small barn. On the other side a road leads to a car parking area with a number of German vehicles sitting on the hardstanding. From there you would only have a short route to the front of the building. A third road seems to lead a distance away behind a number of trees but a small path can also be seen emerging from them to the front of main house.

You need to decide your next move. Do you route to the barn which would give access to the rear of the chateau? Or do you route to the hardstanding with the other vehicles? Or do you steer round to the back of the trees? Decide now,

The barn – **284**

The hardstanding beside the house – **404**

The trees – **464**

265

You tell the guard that having just come from the General, the guard would be wise not to search you and aggravate one of the General's favourite auxiliaries. You flash your eyes knowingly at the guard and tell him it's up to him but really he'll just end up in a lot of trouble. Looking a little agitated the guard says it is the General's policy to search everyone but you can see he's conflicted. There's little to do but wait to see if he buys your statement.

Let's hope you're lucky and picked a soldier who doesn't know his duty.

Choose either **285**, **305** or **325**

266

You realise the guard wagon is just up ahead and will contain all the luggage. Setting off at a determined but reasonable pace, you find the wagon and thankfully the guard is not there, presumably being questioned by the Gestapo. You see plenty of cases and choose to hide in a rack in the middle of the piles of valises. You have to hurry and hitch up your skirt, throwing yourself deep within the rack.

Moments later you hear someone enter the wagon and call out in French, for anyone who's hiding to give themselves up as they will be listened to and not simply taken away. You hold your breath as they begin to search through cases, lifting out the odd one here and there, seeking out their enemy. Time and again they call out. Then another German enters the wagon and begins to help with the search. Part of you thinks you will get caught, and if you are caught hiding then you will be taken away and interrogated. But you could also pretend to be a spooked American instead. After all they are likely to find you anyway.

Do you climb out and give yourself up, and show your papers – **426**

Stay hidden and ride your luck – **466**

267

That's correct. Well done. Now use Number E, Number F and left or right from the middle of your code to generate another page number and go there. If it makes no sense then go to **292**. Goto your next page now.

268

Racing this way and that between the trees you hear several shots ping off them. But you don't stop and soon you are clear of the forest and leaving those in pursuit behind. Once back out in the open you manage to cut through the back of a farmhouse and hide in a gulley until dark.

At the farmhouse that night, the gathered resistance marvel when you walk calmly in after midnight. There is little joy however as your new arrival and one of their friends are dead. The farm owner hides you in the barn and you don't come out for several weeks. Once it is obvious they have given up looking for you and don't know your face, you resume your chores at the barn. You feel sick about what happened but there's a war to win and you must go on to the next challenge. Go there now **- 003**

269

As you drive up to the east gate you realise that there are an unusually large amount of Germans here. You see that vehicles are being stopped and the occupants questioned, maybe due to your escape. You know you have to make a charge through the gate and you put the accelerator right down and the van gives its all. As you approach, the Germans see your intent and there is a sudden hail of bullets coming your direction. You keep ploughing on but it is too much and soon one hits your head leaving you with nothing but darkness.

You have failed. Not a great choice of gate. Try again at 001.

270

You check out the green plant in the corner that sits in a rather ornate pot. But you can see something metallic sticking out of the soil. On closer inspection you find it is a glass cutting tool, which may be useful later. You pocket it and then give the rest of the plant a closer look but find nothing else. (*The search took you 1 min*)

Return to **131** and choose another option

Or has time gone for you, in which case – **376**

271

You approach the bridge from the shadows and can see two men waiting on it. They are dressed in typical French clothing and seem to be waiting for something. However it is almost one in the morning and this seems an unusual hour to be waiting on the bridge for anything. You know that you will be getting into a dinghy and then out along the river to the sea and a rendezvous with a British vessel. But who are these men? Is one your contact? All you know is you are to meet a man with a dinghy. The plans were made so quickly, they hadn't even got the man with the dinghy organised when you departed on mission. Do you,

Approach the first man on the bridge – **291**

Approach the second man on the bridge – **351**

Skirt past the bridge and try to get down to the river – **451**

272

You are still working hard and looking for help when the door bursts open. It is the Commandant and on seeing you, he draws a pistol and demands you put your hands up. Calling for some guards, he has you taken away and placed in a van downstairs with a bag over your head.

After a short journey, you are deposited into a cell and the bag removed. This turns out to be your home for the next three months as you are interrogated. Every day there are questions and pain until one bright morning you are lead to a wall in a field and face a squad of German soldiers. This is where your war ends, another hero lost in a foreign field.

You have failed. Your thoughts and actions were not quick enough. Try again at 001.

273

Carefully you pull the handle of the top drawer and find some combs and hair grease. There are also small clipping scissors for nails and nose hair trimming. The General is obviously a well-groomed man.

On pulling out the second drawer you see an array of socks and briefs and rummage amongst them quietly. At the bottom you discover a key with a blue label attached to it. You pocket it and gently replace the drawer. (*Your search took 2 mins.*) You need to keep moving so where to next?

Return to **233** and look elsewhere.

Or has time gone for you, in which case – **376**

274

You find your sidecar still covered in branches and take it out. You also put your outrider's outfit on again and get ready to set off for the front gate. Suddenly there is a great number of shouts and yells coming from the chateau and the barn.

Did you take out the electrics – **314**

If not, there are a large number of lights coming on all around the grounds, soldiers shouting and cries of a thief. You shake a little but you don't have that far to go to the gate. You could make a break for it trusting that you can beat the communication arriving there. Do you,

Go as quick as you can stopping for no one – **294**

Drive out slowly, gauging what is happening – **354**

275

So what are you going to do? Do you still have time left? Do you,

Examine the Commandant's desk -**295**

Examine the china hutch – **300**

Examine the large globe in the corner – **073**

Examine the chaise longue – **093**

Examine the filing cabinet – **113**

Go to the windows at the front of the room and look out – **153**

Untie the prisoner – **173**

Try to unlock the door – **193**

Or is your time up – **272**

276

Is it a key that you obtained from the kitchen – **296**

Otherwise – **316**

277

You start to say hello and the chef looks strangely at your companion. You explain that you are looking for the washing but the chef's eyes don't move off the airman. Then he begins to shout for the guards and the British airman races forward jumping at him and knocking him to the ground. With a swift blow, the chef is knocked out and your ally rises to his feet. His face though is full of concern and you both look towards the door of the kitchen. There was lot of shouting in the Commandant's room which may have disguised what happened here but it really is pot luck as to whether you have gotten away with it.

You check the landing. What do you see? It's out of your hands because of the noise you've made. So either,

Look here – **377**

Or here – **397**

278

The following morning it is decided you are the best person to make contact as your arrival may be running somewhat scared and need the reassurance of someone who can not only speak English, but be able to identify places at home. After last night's botched drop, you eagerly step forward and begin to assume the disguise you hold of the mute farm worker. It would be normal for you to be in town and to drift around would be atypical of someone out on what is an extremely sunny day.

Your arrival has a code word to drop into conversation in French, the Swiss capital Bern. It certainly is not a word mentioned much in the town and it should give clarification that this will be your person. As you dress a female resistance fighter tells you that several German soldiers are missing including their uniforms and that maybe the arrival will be disguised as a German. Of course, if it were you, there are any number of disguises you could take on and if you stole a peasant person's clothing then it wouldn't be noticed. You are also unaware of the sex of your person so you are determined to keep an open mind on who it may be.

Setting off in the middle of the morning, armed with an empty basket on your arm, you wander into town with a list in hand of foodstuffs to purchase. You are on an errand run from your employer and this will make a good cover with which to wander the town and riverbank.

The stunning weather makes the walk into town pleasant if hot, and you are glad to have a small canteen with you to drink water from. After going to a few different shops and purchasing items off your list by pointing at them, you walk out towards the river which runs through the town and more specifically, towards the riverbank. There's a path that winds along with the river and you can see along it quite easily.

There seems to be four people in the general vicinity of the alternative rendezvous point. One is a German soldier, strangely a little out of the way of their normal places of patrol and also seeming somewhat lost. Further along there is an old woman, hobbling with a stick and dressed in mourning black. Further along, sitting on the bank and watching the water is a peasant man. He seems rather aimless and basks in the sun. And behind all of these holding a bottle of wine is a beggar, dressed in rags and sitting with a small cap in front of him. He seems rather drunk and occasionally shouts out to no one.

You need to get closer to assess which one could be your new arrival. Do you,

Go to the German soldier - **298**

Walk to the old woman - **358**

Go to the peasant man - **418**

Walk past all of these and visit the beggar - **009**

279

You tell the guard it is personal, family correspondence, and that you may be required to type up responses. The guard nods and tells you that he sees this a lot but usually a different girl each time. However he says he doubts you will have much work to do as the General is intending to be at a staff meeting at 5am and normally likes a good hour to prepare himself.

You nod and thank him for the information, saying you'll be as long as the General needs you. He smiles at you seemingly satisfied with your answers.

You are about to climb the stairs but at this point mark down in the notes section at the back of the book that you have 60 mins of time to operate before the guard will become suspicious. In the following passages you will be advised when to deduct time and what to do if time runs out.

Good luck and goto **419**

280

You try the hairpin from the bathroom but it doesn't seem to work in any of the drawers. (*You spend 6 mins trying all the drawers.*)

Do you have other keys or a hairpin to try – **456**

Or has time gone for you, in which case – **376**

If not return to **416** and choose another option

281

Now that you are here, this doesn't seem to be such a good plan and you can see why Headquarters said this was a dangerous area. Before you on the beach are many fences and barricades and who knows what else, all this before you even get to the concrete bunkers above with the German snipers on the lookout. But what other choices do you have? You could go back into the sea and try to make it to the cliffs. It's a dangerous route and there's no guarantee of success. There's a chance of skirting round the beach to the cliffs but you would have to avoid the German patrols that no doubt frequent this area.

It looks like you are in a tough spot but then that's when your spy instincts need to come into play, so what will you do?

Make a run for it straight across the beach – **301**

Go back to the sea and route towards the cliffs – if you came ashore in the dinghy **181,** if you swam ashore **081**

Skirt round the beach to the cliffs hoping to dodge the patrols – **341**

282

You proceed to the wood with a small team and watch closely to see if there are any Germans around. It looks like there are only light patrols in this part and you have no difficulty in placing your explosives and getting your detonators ready. The train then arrives bang on time and you destroy the track just before it arrives causing it to stop abruptly. Unfortunately the train doesn't roll off the tracks but comes up short.

As you watch from the shadows, there is an officer coming off the train with a radio operator. All of a sudden there seems to be a lot of troops deployed off the train and who start to take up protective flanking positions. You think this a little strange as you would actually expect them to go hunting for perpetrators but instead they seem to be securing a nearby road and the train.

All becomes clear when you see a Gestapo car arrive in a convoy and a prisoner emerges from the car in the centre. From the car at the rear two resistance fighters jump out and try to attack those guarding the prisoner but they are cut down by a hail of bullets. The train starts up and you join your resistance team in storming it and trying to free the prisoner. But there are so few of you, most of the team being in town that you are soon shot and the rescue fails miserably.

You have failed. Maybe you made a tactical error. Try again at 001.

283

You say "Hello" to the Frenchman and he responds asking if you are resistance. You say that you are just a friend who is looking for a prisoner. He points across the way but you shake your head. You know your goal is not a simple airman but someone more important. You ask was there anyone else here. He says yes, that a man was in the far cell beside him, but that they took him upstairs to see the big boss quite recently.

The man then begs you to take him with you. He fears they will shoot him soon. He was caught stealing food from a German unit and they have locked him up in here and tried to interrogate him. But he knows nothing and now he fears they have little use for him and he wants to escape. He is quite agitated as he tells you he has a wife and family who don't know where he is. Do you,

Have the vials of acid and wish to use them to release this prisoner – **483**

Have a key and wish to release the prisoner – **008**

Or do you, apologise to the prisoner but say you have nothing to release him with and then

Talk to the British Pilot – **303**

Check the chalkboard on the wall - **488**

284

You remember the gate keeper said that the sidecars were kept in the barn and so decide you should park there. A rider is walking out of the barn as you pull into it and a dim light gives you just enough to see by so that you can park up your vehicle. The other rider has walked off by the time you have parked the sidecar and dismounted. Quickly you stride to the barn entrance and look around for any other German activity. Everything seems quiet and this could be an opportunity to shed your outrider disguise for that of the German auxiliary. Do you,

Change now – **304**

Remain in outrider disguise until you are in the chateau – **384**

285

He's not buying your story and begins to search you. Quickly he discovers the plans and it's curtains for you. He takes you out of the chateau and holds you at gunpoint until a van arrives. The plans are taken from you and you are covered with a black hood.

You wake up in a cell and from there you suffer three months of questioning and torture. Then on a sunny, crisp morning you are led away to a small wall, accompanied by six soldiers and an officer. There you are shot by firing squad, another hero who falls on a foreign shore.

You have failed. Plans really need to be less flippant. Try again at 001.

286

You grab the shoulder of the Frenchman spinning him around and plant a kiss onto his lips. You feel him begin to move away from your grasp and you continue to kiss him, knowing that should he act like this was unwelcome then you would be under the greatest suspicion. You don't know this man but you have made him part of your plan. I guess you must think you are lucky. Choose now!

Goto **366**

Or goto **386**

287

The man looks strangely at you as you explain another officer has told you to come here. He says that this is not normal and takes your hand insisting you come and show him which officer sent you here. This is not going well. Do you,

Comply and follow him – **217**

Attack the man with your hands – **178**

Attack the man with the garden hoe – **198**

288

More speed and you'll get away quicker. The reasoning seems simple, the intent good.
Unfortunately the spray of bullets that comes your way says different and you don't even feel your body hit the ground.

You have failed. Maybe a bit of cover would help next time. Try again at 001.

289

As you drive up to the west gate you realise that you are in luck as there are only a small amount of Germans here. They are stopping vehicles but you wait until they are all occupied and then drive hard towards the gate. By the time they have reacted you have smashed through the gate and are heading along the road. The pursuit is slow in coming and you are able to turn into a side road where a car pulls up alongside you.

You get out of the van and get your prisoner from the rear, and together with the airman you get into the resistance car and speed off. You are dropped off behind your farmhouse base and you wave goodbye to the prisoner and airman who the resistance will now move on.

Telling London that night on the radio of a successful mission is a joy but you know you will not have to wait long before the next mission arrives.

Goto **005**

290

The room is extremely functional with a radio at a table just as you come into the room, and a typist desk complete with typewriter and paper at the rear of the room. There are a number of books beside the radio and a small key cabinet on the wall. There is a window high up but it looks out of reach. The whole room looks well used and you notice that all the paper and books are kept tidy. (*This initial look uses up 1 min of your time. Only deduct this if this is your first time in this room*) Do you,

Examine the typing desk – **310**

Check out the radio – **330**

Look at the books – **370**

Go to the small key cabinet – **390**

Or you may decide there's nothing more to see here. If so you can, return to the landing and

Look around the landing for any help – **439**

Try the door that says "General's Office" – **479**

Try the door that says "Meeting Room" - **077**

Try the unmarked door – **356**

Or has time gone for you, in which case – **376**

291

You walk up to the first man on the bridge who nods at you and then says good morning in French. You try to point to the plans you have but he refuses and motions towards the riverbank. You can see the other man now becoming interested in what you are doing. This first man is now agitated and is starting to push you in the direction of the riverbank.

You see the second man now pull a pistol from his jacket and you begin to run. You hear a gunshot behind you and run for the riverbank. The man you were speaking to now cries out and you think he's been shot causing you to run harder.

Did you injure your leg in a fall from a train – **311**

If not – **331**

292

You spin the dial hopeful of release from the room but as you move it you sense something is wrong. A dart flies out from the lock and strikes you in the neck. You start to feel weary and sick. Everything starts to spin and you collapse onto the floor.

You wake up in a cell and have no idea where you are. This turns out to be your home for the next three months as you are interrogated. Every day there are questions and pain until one bright morning you are lead to a wall in a field and face a squad of German soldiers. This is where your war ends, another hero lost in a foreign field.

You have failed. Your code breaking skills are not what you thought they were. Try again at 001.

293

You lift up the photograph and find it is in a strange frame. Whilst the front of it has a glass cover, the actual frame is sealed at the back and would require a screwdriver to remove the various screws that are keeping the rear secured to the main frame. You give the frame a small shake and can hear something moving inside. What could be kept hidden away in something like this? And how could you access it? Do you?

Throw the frame on the ground to try and crack it? – **313**

Do you have a glass cutter – **333**

Push the front of the frame against the dressing table edge – **353**

Or put the photograph back and return to **233** and look elsewhere (*However this search will have taken you 1 min*)

Or has time gone for you, in which case – **376**

294

You open the throttle up on the sidecar and race down the hill towards the front gate. You see lights coming on all around the chateau but as yet there are few at the gate. You decide this is a good sign and you can see only a single wooden barrier is there to prevent your escape, the gate only being closed on the entrance side and not the exit.

As you speed towards the barrier, you see a guard coming out of the guard hut and waving his arms but he seems unprepared and you knock him flying with the side of the vehicle and then smash through the flimsy wooden barrier that's in place.

Behind, you hear cries and shouts to follow that sidecar but you don't care and have raced away to a side road within five minutes to find a car waiting there with the keys in it. The resistance have come through again. You now face the trek back to England but at least you are clear of the chateau with a fighting chance. Goto **434**

295

There are a number of papers on the Commandant's desk in German but they seem to be of little relevance and you quickly look for other things. There are locked drawers on the right hand side of the desk, three in total. These may hold something useful but it will be hard to force them.

Do you want to try open the drawers, or maybe just one of them – **335**

Do you want to look at something else in the room – **315**

296

You try different keys from the loop of keys you obtained in the kitchen. The door opens after the third try and you step cautiously inside. (*Take 1 min off your time*).

Goto **290**

Or has time gone for you, in which case – **376**

297

You say hello in French but the chef sees the British airman in his German outfit and immediately stands up straight. The chef announces that lunch will be ready within the hour. The British airman says nothing, and actually seems a little confused. He strolls over to the chef who is looking at you both and his mind seems to be coming to the idea that you are not who you say you are.

The airman has spotted this though and knocks the chef out with a punch to the jaw. Carefully he pulls him behind a table so he cannot be seen from the doorway. You may not have much time to search the kitchen for anything useful. Do you,

Search the larder – **076**

Check the cupboards – **036**

Examine the work surfaces – **056**

Leave and go back to the landing – **016**

298

With a rifle over his shoulder, the German soldier stands and smokes, looking around at the scenery. He gives your figure a quick glance as you walk up to him but then turns away. It is certainly unusual that he is here all alone and not close by any other soldier but you know it's not impossible. However if this is your arrival then this scenario is definitely a possibility.

Being disguised as a mute you don't want to talk first but your arrival won't know that you are, so you are going to have to speak if you want to talk to them. Do you,

Engage in conversation – **318**

Try to subtlety get the soldier to follow you to somewhere quiet – **338**

Leave the soldier and instead, if you haven't already,

Talk to the old woman – **358**

The peasant man -**418**

The Beggar -**009**

299

You tell the guard that you have been requested by the General for some urgent typing. He nods saying to you that it wouldn't be the first time the General has gotten up in the middle of the night to dictate something. However he rarely lasts more than a half hour before he wants to go back to sleep. You thank him and he steps aside to let you on your way.

You are about to climb the stairs but at this point mark down in the notes section at the back of the book that you have 45 mins of time to operate before the guard will become suspicious. In the following passages you will be advised when to deduct time and what to do if time runs out.

Good luck and goto **419**

300

There are a large number of plates and crockery in the china hutch, including a collection of dinky tea pots from around the world. There appears to be nothing of any military connection and certainly nothing of use unless you want to make a cup of tea. I mean, what did you expect here?

You have wasted 2 minutes looking. If the British airman is with you, you searched quicker and only wasted 1 minute.

Goto **275**

301

Gathering your breath, you launch out from the barricade, running hard ahead, seeing that first fence and preparing to dive down beside it and work out a way over. The last thing you hear is a click, and then an almighty bang. The snipers in the concrete bunkers scan the beach after the explosion but they don't see anyone running anymore.

You failed but at least you went out with a bang. To retry goto 001

302

You proceed to the wood with the bulk of your team and watch closely to see if there are any Germans around. It looks like there are only light patrols in this part and you have no difficulty in placing your explosives and getting your detonators ready. The train then arrives bang on time and you destroy the track just before it arrives causing it to stop abruptly. Unfortunately the train doesn't roll off the tracks but comes up short.

As you watch from the shadows, there is an officer coming off the train with a radio operator. All of a sudden there seems to be a lot of troops deployed off the train and who start to take up protective flanking positions. You think this a little strange as you would actually expect them to go hunting for perpetrators but instead they seem to be securing a nearby road and the train.

All becomes clear when you see a Gestapo car arrive in a convoy and a prisoner emerges from the car in the centre. You can see that you have failed in your mission to disable the train and they want to put him on the train at this point. Without hesitation, you call out to your team to attack and secure the prisoner. It's a wild attack with no planning but you do have an element of surprise.

You had hoped that the small team might have shown up in a Gestapo car but they don't appear and you are taking heavy fire. You need to concentrate your fire somewhere. Do you,

Shoot up the train – **322**

Attack the cars – **342**

Aim at the exchange? – **362**

303

You step up to the cell and see a moustached man scratching something onto the wall with a piece of stone. He turns to look at you and you recognise the Royal Air Force uniform. He looks somewhat surprised that a maid is here but then turns back to scraping something onto the wall. Do you,

Speak to him in English – **323**

Speak to him in French – **343**

Decide to talk instead to the Peasant if you haven't already – **283**

Look at the other cells if you haven't already – **263**

Check the chalkboard on the wall if you haven't already - **488**

304

Without hesitation, you remove the outrider jacket and trousers, folding down your skirt and letting your hair hang loose behind you. You are looking slightly rough and ready but this is the disguise for inside the chateau. Who knows when you will have another chance to change? You calmly hide the clothes in the barn and then walk easily across the path towards the chateau.

As you start walking, a German officer spots you and tells you to halt. You do so standing to attention as you notice his higher rank. He strides over and looks you up and down. Then he asks you in German why you were in the barn, as what purpose would you have in the parking area for sidecars.

Do you,

Tell him you are a mechanic and you were correcting a fault on one of the vehicles – **324**

Tell him a senior officer requested you attend the barn and try to look embarrassed – **344**

Tell him you were feeling unwell and needed a stroll – **364**

305

He's not buying your story and begins to search you. Quickly he discovers the plans and it's curtains for you. He takes you out of the chateau and holds you at gunpoint until a van arrives. The plans are taken from you and you are covered with a black hood.

You wake up in a cell and from there you suffer three months of questioning and torture. Then on a sunny, crisp morning you are led away to a small wall, accompanied by six soldiers and an officer. There you are shot by firing squad, another hero who falls on a foreign shore.

You have failed. Plans really need to be less flippant. Try again at 001.

306

You smile politely as the Gestapo officer arrives. He demands your papers in German. You catch yourself from answering and look at him bewilderedly. "French or English, please" you ask in French. "Ah, English," he says. "American," you reply quickly, and he asks for your papers in English. Handing them over you smile again and look around at the number of troops at the station. It would seem the Germans are looking for someone and you hope it's not you.

But the officer seems confused and asks why you have left the train? Do you,

Run – **326**

Tell him you needed some air – **346**

307

You reply that you are just sorting the washing and then turn to it and grab one of the shirts. He tells you to make sure that you get those rust stains out properly as he looks over your shoulder. He then pinches your bottom before walking away. Do you,

Let him leave – **098**

Attack him from behind – **118**

308

It's not great cover but at least it is some sort of cover. You half run, half crouch and make reasonable progress as you head this way and that. There are bullets ripping through the stalks and you feel like this escape is turning into a bit of a lottery. It is, but how lucky are you?

Goto **328**, **348** or **368**

309

As you drive up to the north gate you realise that this is the main gate and as such there are a large amount of Germans here. You see that vehicles are being stopped and questioned, maybe due to your escape. You know you have to make a charge through the gate and you put the accelerator right down and the van gives its all. As you approach, the Germans see your intent and there is a sudden hail of bullets coming your direction. You keep ploughing on but it is too much and soon one hits your head leaving you with nothing but darkness.

You have failed. Not a great choice of gate. Try again at 001.

310

You notice that the typewriter is similar to the one you used when going through your training and it brings a sentimental thought during this pressure situation you are in. You check the paper beside the typewriter but it is all blank and neatly stacked as if it is a fresh ream. *(It has taken you 1 min to complete this examination)* There's nothing more to see here.

Return to **290** and choose another option

Or has time gone for you, in which case – **376**

311

You drag your leg as quick as you can and as you round the corner of the bridge you can see a small dinghy awaiting you. But as terrified as you are and despite the adrenalin pumping through your veins, your leg slows you down. Another gunshot rings out and you fall to the ground. Your last image is of the plans being taken from you.

You have failed. You couldn't have gotten any closer. Try again at 001.

312

If you haven't untied the prisoner you do this now.

You grab hold of the prisoner and support his weight as he makes drowsy steps. With the door open you think about escape and what to do with the prisoner.

There are certainly options to think about. Ultimately you need to get outside the compound which is being watched by the resistance. If you can get clear and are not being pursued you will be picked up somehow by them. But that seems a long way off.

You think through your options:

You could make a run for it to the perimeter on foot – **332**

If you have looked out the windows upstairs – **170**

If you have been in the store downstairs – **369**

313

You throw the frame to the ground and hear a satisfying crack. Reaching down you carefully pick away at the glass and then reach in to remove the photograph. But someone has stirred due to the noise from your actions. The General has awoken and doesn't wait to ask you questions but instead shoots the intruder in his room. You are a fallen hero forever lost on a foreign field.

You have failed. Loud actions when sneaking around doesn't always work. Goto 001 to try again.

314

There are lots of cries but no lights come on and you realise that your sabotage of the electrics was successful. Communications will be slow as well and so you open the throttle up on the sidecar and race down the hill towards the front gate. There are no lights down the hill and you can see only a single wooden barrier is there to prevent your escape, the gate only being closed on the entrance side and not the exit.

As you speed towards the barrier, you see a guard coming out of the guard hut and waving his arms but he seems unprepared and you knock him flying with the side of the vehicle and then smash through the flimsy wooden barrier that's in place.

Behind, you hear cries and shouts to follow that sidecar but you don't care and have raced away to a side road to find a car waiting there with the keys in it. The resistance have come through again. You now face the trek back to England but at least you are clear of the chateau with a fighting chance. Goto **434**

315

Looking through the papers and then at the drawers took 2 minutes of your time. Cross the time off and then goto **275**

316

You try your keys but alas none fit. You try and jiggle them about but to no avail. (*After 2 mins you stop realising these keys are not correct.*)

Go back to **216** and choose another option.

Or has time gone for you, in which case – **376**

317

You say hello to the chef and he spins around to regard you suspiciously. He asks what you are doing here and you reply that you are looking for some laundry. You can tell he doesn't believe you as he begins to ask how long you have been working here. You approach him while you answer and grab a bottle without him noticing off the kitchen top. When he turns away to look for a list of maids, you bring the bottle down on the back of his head. He falls unconscious to the floor. You drag him off to the corner of the kitchen and tie him up as best you can with some kitchen cord.

You have a chance to examine the kitchen but you need to be quick. Do you,

Search the larder – 076

Check the cupboards – 036

Examine the work surfaces – 056

Leave and go back to the landing – 016

318

You stroll up to the German telling him how handsome he looks in his uniform. You see him smile and look at you intently before replying in broken French that you look delightful. He asks what you are doing here today and you show him your basket, advising him you are shopping for your employer at the farm.

You see his face become puzzled and he stares at you even harder. Then he grabs your arm and begins to drag you away. He's strong and you cannot stop him from holding onto you. He takes you round another corner where he sees another German soldier. He calls him over in German and you begin to sweat as you hear him ask in their language, was the farm girl out of town not a mute.

Suddenly they are both looking at you and his friend calls a van over to you. You are put in the back of the vehicle and a bag is placed over your head. When you are next allowed to see, you are in a prison cell.

Days of questions and torture follow until that fateful day they lead you to a simple white room with a guillotine. You never see England again, another fallen hero on a foreign shore. But the worst thought is that you know the farm would have been raided too and you wonder if anyone else survived.

You have failed. Who knows where the new arrival ended up but not staying in cover cost you your life. You can try again at 001.

319

You tell the guard that you need access to the documents upstairs. He looks at you suspiciously and asks if you mean the main office. You nod and he tells you that the General doesn't like anyone up there after hours when he is asleep. It is clear that you are hitting a brick wall with this request. Do you,

Tell the guard you screwed up and that you need to get some paperwork and correct it before the morning or there will be hell to pay – **339**

Tell him the General gave out a special request to you to come and complete it only ten minutes ago – **359**

320

You sit in the room and drink some of the water from the jug beside your bed. Time passes slowly but after a half hour there is a knock on your door. You ask who it is and a man's voice replies saying he requires to see again your papers. This doesn't look good and you make for the window and hopefully an escape onto some lower roofs. Alas there is a German soldier there already.

The door is broken open and you see the same officer who examined your papers at the station. He smiles horribly and more soldiers come from behind him taking you and your case away.

You are taken to a prison where you are questioned and tortured for three weeks. Then one day you are taken out in the early morning sunshine with a firing squad. In the glorious early dawn you become another fallen hero on a foreign field.

You have failed. Sometimes you need to take more positive action. Try again at 001.

321

It's almost too easy for them as they see your feet sticking out from the barricade. The German guard issues you an instruction to stand in German and you do. That makes them think you are a spy despite your protests in your best French. They take you away to a cell where you have to explain yourself over the coming week. But they don't believe you and you are treated as a spy, one who never sees the end of the war or her homeland again. Still at least you didn't know anything so you had nothing to tell them.

You failed. Goto 001 to start again. Lucky you, real spies don't get that chance.

322

You shout at your men to fire at the windows of the train and the glass begins to explode. You see the main officer in charge yell at the guards to take the prisoner away from the train and to get him back in the car. Soon they drive off quickly but you think you spot a new Gestapo car that drives off in convoy with the others.

Retreating back to the farmhouse, you wait for news from the small team you sent to town. When they walk into the house at dawn your team is heartened, especially when they say that they managed to follow the convoy of Gestapo cars and have the location of the prisoner.

After a small celebration glass of homemade liquor, your team splits up to get some sleep while others in the resistance are tasked with getting as much information about the new location as they can. You however need to get some sleep as you will be called into action later that night when you attempt to spring the prisoner from jail.

Goto **004**

323

You say hello in English and he looks at you suspiciously. He asks who you are and you tell him you are looking for a prisoner of some importance. He says that the only other prisoner was taken upstairs very recently but wonders if you have a key to the cell.

As a combatant it's his duty to escape, or he could even cause a diversion, if your prisoner is important enough. His eyes are full of hope as he waits for your reply. Do you,

Tell him you haven't anything to open the cell with – **363**

If you have one, open the cell with a key – **383**

If you have the vials open the door with one – **403**

324

You tell him you are a mechanic and you were attending to a broken sidecar. He looks at you, eyes full of doubt and then comes behind you and pulls his pistol out and places it into your back. He tells you there are no female mechanics on site and that you are clearly lying. He marches you to the chateau where you are taken to a room and interrogated. Over the coming days you succumb to their methods and recount the full extent of your mission. You are then removed to a distant prison.

A month later, having extracted all the information from you they can, the Germans take you outside on a clear morning and line you up before a firing squad. Your mission ends as another fallen hero on distant shores.

You have failed. You went off script and got caught out. Try again at 001.

325

He looks at you and says okay but that it is a secret between you and him. He can't be seen to be disregarding his duty. You step forward and kiss him on the cheek, telling him he's a wise boy. You need to keep moving. Did you enter the building by the kitchen or the front entrance? Best to go back the way you came as you'll know what to expect? Did you,

Enter via the kitchen initially – **058**

Enter via the front entrance – **078**

326

You run as fast as you can away from the officer, afraid that your papers and story won't hold up. But you don't get very far as he lets out a cry demanding that you are shot in German. You don't see who shoots you and everything ends.

You have failed. Maybe a little trust in your story might have been in order. If you want to try again goto 001.

327

You tell him in an angry voice that you don't question orders and that even if it is the middle of the night you report as required and he should stop getting in the way. He seems chastened and nods his head saying he will just go back to sleep. You tell him that's a wise thing to do as the General won't appreciate you being delayed.

You have to route direct to the hallway beyond the kitchen and you hear him lightly snoring as you reach it.

Goto **200**

328

Goto **368**

329

You route to the rear door in an attempt to sneak round to the laundry van. You will have to be quick and you hope for the best as you drag this half beaten down man with you. It's a fool's hope really taking him like this and that becomes evident as you run into some German guards. They look at you first and smile but then ask to see the person hidden by all the sheets. They think it's another maid but then they realise it's the prisoner. You are taken away and placed in a van with a bag over your head.

After a short journey, you are deposited into a cell and the bag removed. This turns out to be your home for the next three months as you are interrogated. Every day there are questions and pain until one bright morning you are led to a wall in a field and face a squad of German soldiers. This is where your war ends, another hero lost in a foreign field.

You have failed. Not the greatest plan. Try again at 001.

330

The radio set sits dark with no lights illuminated on it. It looks like a standard German issue model and no doubt for when the General wants messages broadcast in a hurry. You can see the on switch and dial and wonder if you can hear any local chatter on the airwaves. Or is it best not to mess about with the controls. *(It has taken you 1 min to complete this examination)* Do you,

Switch on the radio – **350**

Leave the radio alone, in which case return to **290** and choose another option.

Or has time gone for you, in which case – **376**

331

You run hard, gunshots ringing behind you. As you round the corner of the bridge, you can see a dinghy in the water. Two men are inside and they begin to fire shots back at the man following you. You dive into the water and swim hard in your jacket and dress. But you realise the men on the dinghy have stopped firing. Soon they are pulling you on board and you sit there with the plans. The man on the bridge has been shot and there will be Germans coming soon without a doubt. But your sailors are strong and soon the dinghy is heading out to sea from the river, under cover of darkness.

Goto **489**

332

If you have met the Chef – **352**

Otherwise read on:

You drag the prisoner down the stairs and head back out the initial door you came in. You realise there's a lot of open ground up ahead and you wonder if you can make it.

If you have been in the Store and the Boiler – **432**

If you haven't and the British airman is with you – **452**

Otherwise – **472**

333

You take the glass cutter from the meeting room and carefully cut out the glass front. Removing it, you then take out the photograph of the child and find a piece of paper inside which you open up. It has a code inside that reads *14 93 42*. You wonder what this could be for but not for too long as there is more to do. (*Your actions have taken you 2 mins.*)

Return now to **233** and search elsewhere

Or has time gone for you, in which case – **376**

334

You open the throttle up on the sidecar and race down the hill towards the front gate. You see lights coming on all around the chateau but as yet there are few at the gate. You decide this is a good sign and you can see only a single wooden barrier is there to prevent your escape, the gate only being closed on the entrance side and not the exit.

However you are quite some distance away and as you speed towards the barrier, you see a guard coming out of the guard hut and with an automatic rifle in his hands. He opens fire peppering you with bullets. You are not conscious for the crash and become another fallen hero on a foreign field.

You have failed. And yet you were so close. Try again at 001.

335

Do you have a lock pick – **355**

Do you have the British airman with you – **375**

If not – **395**

336

You take the hair clip from the bathroom and try it on the lock. It takes a bit of fiddling but the door opens. (*It takes you 2 mins, so deduct this from your time.*)

Enter the room now at **290**

Or has time gone for you, in which case – **376**

337

You say hello to the chef in German and he stops chopping and looks up at you with a little surprise.

Do you have the British airman with you? If so, is he in his British uniform – **357,** or is he in a German uniform – **417**

Or are you alone – **437**

338

You smile approaching the soldier and you watch him smile back at you. You swing your hips in a feminine way and gently try to call him to follow you with your hand. Although he smiles again, he then simply lights another cigarette and stands there watching the area around him.

He doesn't seem to be looking for anyone in particular but then again that may be your new arrival in disguise. Or he could simply be a German soldier. Either way this ploy to get him to follow you isn't working. Do you,

Engage in conversation – **318**

Leave the soldier and instead, if you haven't already,

Go to the old woman – **358**

The peasant man – **418**

The Beggar -**009**

339

He looks at you with a fondness and says he is always happy to help out such a pretty girl. But he warns you that you can't make a noise and that he can only afford you a short while. The General won't be happy if he gets up and finds you still there. You nod and say thanks, giving him a peck on the cheek. He steps aside to let you up the stairs.

You are about to climb the stairs but at this point mark down in the notes section at the back of the book that you have 45 mins of time to operate before the guard will become suspicious. In the following passages you will be advised when to deduct time and what to do if time runs out.

Good luck and goto **419**

340

The ottoman has a plush cover and you try to lift the top of it up finding that it swings open quite easily for you. Inside there are a number of sheets, all laid out neatly. You lift a few up and find them to be of good quality and strong. Your hands rummage through the sheets but there is nothing else in the ottoman so you replace everything carefully.

Return to **213** and choose another option (*Deduct 2 mins for the time you were searching*)

Or has time gone for you, in which case – **376**

341

Racing off into the dark you realise how risky this is. Patrols don't always shine torches where they go and you struggle to pick out figures in the dark. There are also snipers watching the beach from the bunkers at the top of the cliffs and surely it will be pot luck if they don't see you at times, especially as you have to cross open beach.

But there's nothing else for it, as to stay where you are will definitely lead to capture and a prison cell at best. So you press on, racing across the beach before you hear a sound. You dive behind a metal barricade which gives little protection. You can hear men talking, in German, but it is hushed and appears to be orders, a leader telling his men to be vigilant. How vigilant will they be? Will you be lucky? Because luck is all you seem to have here.

Test your luck and go to one of these numbers **361**, **321** or **381**

342

You shout at your men to attack the Gestapo cars and you see the guards and the prisoner run for cover. As the glass flies up from the cars, you hear the train start up and you decide to close in on the cars to find your target. Your team is taking heavy fire for the soldiers on the train and from those at the Gestapo cars.

But then you look towards the train and realise that you have made a mistake. The prisoner is being forced onto the train and it is starting to move. You shout out to your team but it is too late and the train's disappearing. You are now caught in a fire fight and are being closed in on all sides. It isn't long before you succumb to the sheer weight of firepower being concentrated on you.

You have failed. Possibly due to a tactical error. Try again at 001.

343

You say hello to the airman in French and he simply looks at you. Again you try and he shrugs his shoulders and opens the palm of his hands. He says to you in English that he cannot understand. This is not working but at least you are still maintaining your cover as a French maid. You'll have to break that if you want to communicate with him. And are you sure about the French man in the cell opposite? It may be worth the risk to glean more information but will you take the risk? Do you,

Speak to the airman in English – **323**

Ignore him and check out the rest of the cell area by doing one of the following if you have not already done so:

Examine the far cells – **263**

Talk to the French Peasant man – **283**

Check the chalkboard on the wall - **488**

Or do you leave the cells and move on to another area:

Enter the room marked "Boiler" – **028**

Retreat back to the stairs and climb them – **144**

Retreat back to the front corridor if you have not been that way before – **064**

344

You force a blush and tell the officer that a more senior officer had requested your presence. When he enquires further, you say that it would be unwise to ask that question as it was a matter of pleasure and not military business. Again you force your face to go red and you avoid eye contact. The officer looks at you and says he cannot fault his superior's choice and then tells you to hurry along to the chateau.

You quickly move off breathing a metaphorical sigh of relief. You walk quickly to the rear of the building and see the kitchen door before you. This may be a good option as you would avoid any interest from the guard on the front door. However, the front door is also only a short walk away. Do you,

Enter via the kitchen door – **484**

Route and enter via the front door – **447**

345

You make your way quickly and quietly to the General's bedroom. Taking the sheets out of the ottoman you tie them together and then take them into the bathroom. Immediately, you open the window and tie the sheets to the bath taps, pulling at them to make sure they are secure.

As you climb out the window you don't look down and descend quickly and elegantly onto the first roof. From there you take a second set of sheets and attach another line to the floor. Soon you are on the ground and ready to make a move to the sidecar. However is there anything you can do to make this move even easier?

Did you read the electrical plans in meeting room – **055**

If not, where is your sidecar parked?

In the barn – **254**

Hidden in the trees in the orchard – **274**

346

You tell him it's because you needed some air and that you will be getting back on when the whistle sounds. He seems content with that answer and hands your papers back.

You continue to stand, ignoring the sweat pouring down your back from the tension and await the train whistle. Once back on board you find your cabin again and sit down again, smiling at the German officer who is still there. The train rumbles on through the countryside.

Goto **206**

347

The chef asks with a yawn what you are doing in the kitchen as outriders are not allowed in here. He seems quite angry as he rises to his full height. Do you,

Tell him not to question you and slap him round the head – **367**

Apologise and leave for kitchen door – **387**

Tell him you're actually on your way to see the General but you are in disguise – **407**

348

Your heart is in your mouth as you run for your life, keeping low so they cannot see where you are going. It feels like the bullets will never stop but they have as you break cover at the end of the field. Beyond is a farm house which you run around before routing into a deep gulley. Hiding there until nightfall, you manage to stay undiscovered and walk to your own base once darkness has fallen.

At the farmhouse that night, the gathered resistance marvel when you walk calmly in after midnight. There is little joy however as your new arrival and one of their friends are dead. The farm owner hides you in the barn and you don't come out for several weeks. Once it is obvious they have given up looking for you and don't know your face, you resume your chores at the barn. You feel sick about what happened but there's a war to win and you must go on to the next challenge. Go there now **- 003**

349

You route to the rear door in an attempt to sneak round to the laundry van. You will have to be quick and you hope for the best as you drag this half beaten down man and the British airman with you. It's a fool's hope really taking them like this and that becomes evident as you run into some German guards. They look at you first and smile but then ask to see the person hidden by all the sheets. They think it's more maids but then they realise one of them is the prisoner. You are taken away and placed in a van with a bag over your head.

After a short journey, you are deposited into a cell and the bag removed. This turns out to be your home for the next three months as you are interrogated. Every day there are questions and pain until one bright morning you are lead to a wall in a field and face a squad of German soldiers. This is where your war ends, another hero lost in a foreign field.

You have failed. Not the greatest plan. Try again at 001.

350

You switch on the radio and turn to the dial but it sends out a piercing whistle before you react and switch it back off. You listen carefully and hear footsteps coming up the stairs. You switch on the light as a guard arrives and tell him you accidentally switched on the radio. He looks dubiously at you when start to tell him how curiosity got the better of you.

He says at least you didn't wake the General and so after warning you to be more careful he says you had better get back to your work. But he seems to also like you and it takes a while to ensure when he has left the room that he has gone downstairs. (*It takes you 10 mins to be sure he's gone, so deduct that from your time left*)

Return to **290** and choose another option

Or has time gone for you, in which case – **376**

351

You approach the second man on the bridge and try to indicate that you have plans with you. He says in a quiet voice that he can take them off you and get you out of here. You are a little unsure but you know you need to hurry. Do you,

Hand the plans to the man – **371**

Tell the man no, you keep the plans – **391**

352

You may want to disguise the prisoner in the Chef's outfit. Presumably the Chef is still knocked out and this would make a better cover than the prisoner's current clothes.

If you wish to do this – **372**

If not return to **332** and read on

353

You push the glass of the photograph against the edge of the table and you think that it is straining but no cracks are observed. You try for a good minute and think something might be happening but in the dark it's difficult to assess the glass. (*This effort so far has cost you 2 mins. Deduct that now.*) Do you,

Keep trying in the hope the glass breaks - **373**

Return now to **233** and search elsewhere

Or has time gone for you, in which case - **376**

354

With a pursuit in progress, you decide to drive slowly down to the front gate and you see lights coming on all around the front gate. However as you arrive at the exit gate, it is still open, although there is a flimsy wooden barrier across it, indicating you should stop.

You bring the sidecar to a halt and a soldier comes out telling you to wait right there as there is trouble afoot. He comes over and asks for your papers and you pass them over without hesitation. You ask what the matter is and he says there has been an intruder and he'll be able to deal with you in a moment.

As you sit there waiting his return, you overhear a calm serene voice talking on the radio to the guard.

Did you steal the code book from the communications room in the chateau - **374**

If not, you wonder what's going on. Is this just a routine message as it's so calm or something sinister? Do you,

Wait for the guard to come out - **394**

Race off right now, smashing the barrier - **414**

355

Looking at the locks, you reckon it will take you a minute to open each lock. There are three drawers, top, middle and bottom. Each time you open one, take a minute off your time. This includes your search time for inside the drawer. Goto **415**

356

The door has a handle and appears to be unlocked. You swing it open gently and can hear snoring from inside. (*This takes 1 min off your time.*) Do you,

Enter – **213**

Or rethink your plans and instead

Look around the landing for any help – **439**

Try the door that says "General's Office" – **479**

Try the door that says "Meeting Room" - **077**

Try the door that says "Communications Room – **216**

Or has time gone for you, in which case – **376**

357

The chef shouts out loudly and you start to panic. He screams out in German for guards and the British airman races forward jumping at him and knocking him to the ground. With a swift blow, the chef is knocked out and your ally rises to his feet. His face though is full of concern and you both look towards the door of the kitchen. There was lot of shouting in the Commandant's room which may have disguised what happened here but it really is pot luck as to whether you have gotten away with it.

You check the landing. What do you see? It's out of your hands because of the noise you've made. So either,

Look here – **377**

Or here – **397**

358

You approach the old woman dressed in black, obviously mourning for a husband or child in her recent past. She carries a simple stick and walks very unsteadily. You offer her a hand for extra support and she grabs it. You don't speak but the woman says thank you in French before explaining that without her son to support her she is having a hard time going anywhere. She then mentions that these days are not like when she was growing up near Bern and goes on to talk about her past.

The accent is certainly not a local accent. But is this your new arrival in disguise? Or did the Germans catch them and this is now a trap? How far do you trust your instincts on this? Do you –

Whisper a quiet word to assure them they are with the right person – **378**

Help the old woman for a few more steps before gracefully saying goodbye – **398**

359

You tell the guard that the General himself called you to get this paperwork corrected only ten minutes ago. The guard points his weapon at you saying the General has been asleep for the last hour as the guard can see all telephone calls being made through the switchboard of the chateau and none was made. He takes you at gunpoint to the front of the building where he finds additional guards.

You are covered with a hood and next find yourself next in a cell. For days you are questioned and tortured, giving up many secrets. After three months you are led away to a wall in a garden where you are shot by firing squad. Your last memory is the sound of birds chirping their morning calls, then rudely interrupted by the crack of gunfire.

You have failed. Embellishing your story may have been a mistake. Goto 001 to try again.

360

With your escapee supported by yourself you don't make a lot of speed and as you head to the main gate you realise it has been closed. The Commandant must have made it back and found the prisoner missing. It's an easy matter for the number of guards at the north gate to spot you and recapture you. You are taken away and placed in a van with a bag over your head.

After a short journey, you are deposited into a cell and the bag removed. This turns out to be your home for the next three months as you are interrogated. Every day there are questions and pain until one bright morning you are led to a wall in a field and face a squad of German soldiers. This is where your war ends, another hero lost in a foreign field.

You have failed. Escaping by the main entrance wasn't so bright. Try again at 001.

361

You must have an angel watching over you because the patrol passes right beside you but not one looks your direction. You shake as they leave the area knowing that your life depended not on your skill but on the whim of some guards. But there's no time to wait, you need to keep going and get to the cliffs. As you leave the beach behind you, you clamber onto the rocks and look for a way up the cliffs ahead.

But maybe your luck is no longer holding as a man steps out wearing a cloth cap, black jacket, grey trousers and black shoes. He has a gun pointed at you and you gulp wondering if he is going to fire. But maybe he's your contact. They have said nothing about what he looks like, only where you would meet him.

But he would have seen the activity on the beach, surely? Maybe this is worth a risk, maybe you need to take a chance. Then again, your luck might just run out. Do you,

Speak the code word given to you by Headquarters for meeting your contact – **201**

Blag a story in French about how you have been abandoned by your boyfriend – **221**

Wait for him to speak- **241**

362

You tell your team to fire at the point of exchange of the prisoner from the Gestapo cars to the train. You see guards falling down and extra soldiers flooding in to fill the gap. There are a mass of bullets reigning in on the small area and then the inevitable happens. You see the prisoner take a bullet and fall to the ground. He doesn't seem to be moving and soon the Germans abandon him on the ground and defend themselves by moving behind fixed barriers.

You try to get your team out by turning around and leaving through the wood but the Germans have mobilised their soldiers, who no longer have a prisoner to defend, and you are cut down in the woods. At least they won't get the information they hoped from the prisoner. But for you and the resistance fighters that you led, the war is over.

You have failed. Maybe an error of judgement as they say. Try again at 001.

363

You tell the man you have nothing to open the doors with and his face falls. He asks that if you do find something then you come back here and help him. You say you'll do what you can, lying to stay on task for your mission. You find it hard to stay now that you have been so blatant with your lies and you have to leave the cell area completely. Sometimes you have to make tough choices but you don't have to like doing it.

You exit the cells and wonder where you'll go next. Do you,

If you haven't already, enter the room marked "Boiler" – **028**

Retreat back to the stairs and climb them – **144**

Retreat back to the front corridor if you have not been that way before – **064**

364

You say you were felling unwell and that you needed a stroll. The officer looks at you concerned as you grab your stomach pretending to be in pain. He says you would be best back in the clerical sleeping quarters but advises that you go via the kitchen door as this way you will avoid any of the staff who may want you for work. After all, he says, not everyone has his caring nature. You nod a thank you and start to make your way towards the kitchen door. But he grabs your arm and walks you there himself.

Leaving you at the door he wishes you a speedy recovery and waits to see you inside. You have no option but to enter through that door.

Do so now – **484**

365

You decide that you can get past the guard by sneaking up on him and then knocking him out. Taking the small bottle of chloroform, you pour a little out into the cloth that was with it and then wrap the cloth up tight. With the bottle secured again, you creep along the landing and try to spy the guard.

He is moving about and so you hide in the shadows at the top of the stairs until he comes to a halt, facing away from you. However he is standing right at the side of the stairs where the carpet doesn't run. The carpet only runs down the middle of the stairs and you are worried that to get close will involve you stepping on wooden boards in your shoes, possibly alerting him. Do you,

Take your shoes off and creep down the wooden outside of the stairs – **385**

Keep your shoes on and risk going down the wooden part of the stairs as you sneak up on him - **405**

Keep your shoes on and stretch towards him from the carpet area – **425**

366

The man seems bemused but then decides that you might be someone he would enjoy and he clenches you tight kissing you now in a romantic fashion. Breaking off only slightly, he begins to tell you in French how delighted he is to see such a beautiful girl and that you really must stop surprising him like this. Again he holds you tight and begins to kiss you, keeping you close as the Gestapo officer approaches. You hear a sharp cough and the Frenchman breaks you apart before turning to the Gestapo officer, with a look of indignation on his face.

There is a stream of words in French at a pace you struggle to keep up with but the general gist of it is that he is annoyed that the moment he has been waiting for has been broken by such an angry looking man. Again and again the man makes a protest until the Gestapo officer stops him with a finger raised to his lips. The Frenchman stops immediately. He is told that in future he must show greater respect and that an outburst like that will not be tolerated.

The Frenchman nods and the Gestapo officer moves away. You continue to hold the hand of this unknown Frenchman until the Gestapo soldiers have moved away and you hear the train's whistle sound. The Frenchman turns to you and indicates the train. "Enchantée," he says and helps you on board. You return to your seat to continue your journey wondering the name of this French patriot.

Goto **206**

367

You tell the man angrily that you shouldn't be questioned by a mere chef and you clip him round the head with your hand. He then jumps you and a fight ensues with food and other kitchen items falling from the storeroom shelves causing a lot of noise. Soon guards arrive and in the ensuing aftermath, you are discovered to be a spy. You are frog marched out to a van and your head covered with a hood.

You are taken away to a nearby prison. After three months of questions and torture you are led to a wall in a field one day with a firing squad. Here your adventure ends, another hero lost on a foreign field.

You have failed. Things made up on the spot sometimes back fire. Goto 001.

368

You think it is going well as bullet after bullet passes by you. But then one hits your head and you catch a brief glimpse of the arriving ground before there is nothing else.

You have failed. Sometimes luck doesn't favour the brave. Try again at 001.

369

Is the British airman with you – **389**

If not - **409**

370

You take a look at the books beside the radio and see they are code books. However the bulk of them need cross referencing to a cypher and without that they are useless to you. However you do see a small book indicating code words used at the chateau to instruct guards where to go in the event of someone infiltrating the site. This you pocket as it may be useful later. (*Your search has taken you 2mins*)

Return to **290** and choose another option

Or has time gone for you, in which case – **396**

371

You quickly give the man the plans and he thanks you. You start to look for the dinghy to take you away but the man has pulled out a gun. He shoots you and leaves the scene quickly. As you spend your last moments on that bridge, you realise you have just given the plans to a German spy.

You have failed. You've been so clever but that was pretty dumb. Try again at 001.

372

How much time did you have remaining when you unlocked the door?

Over 5 mins - **392**

5 mins or less - **412**

373

You continue pushing against the table edge when suddenly you feel the glass crack. It takes a bit of effort to make the glass separate from the frame quietly but you are soon able to take out the photograph. Behind it is a piece of paper which you open up. It has a code inside that reads 14 93 42. You wonder what this could be for but not for too long as there is more to do. (*Your actions have taken you 2 mins.*)

Return now to **233** and search elsewhere

Or has time gone for you, in which case - **376**

374

You recognise the German word used by the voice on the radio and think you saw it in the code book. Quickly checking the code book you realise it means "Lockdown". You toss the code book aside and open the throttle on the sidecar and smash through the barrier out onto the open road beyond.

Behind, you hear cries and shouts to follow that sidecar but you don't care and have raced away to a side road within five minutes to find a car waiting there with the keys in it. The resistance have come through again. You now face the trek back to England but at least you are clear of the chateau with a fighting chance. Goto **434**

375

The British airman thinks he can smash open the drawers with some of the furniture lying around. However it won't be easy and will take 3 minutes for each drawer to be broken open. There are three drawers, top, middle and bottom. Each time you smash one open, take 3 minutes off your time. This includes your search time for inside the drawer. Goto **415**

376

You turn round and realise you are being watched. The guard from downstairs must have come to check up on what you were doing. He believes you were taking too long and now he has a much dimmer view of what you are at. Pointing his gun at you he asks you to come with him. He takes you at gunpoint to the front of the building where he finds additional guards.

You are covered with a hood and next find yourself next in a cell. For days you are questioned and tortured, giving up many secrets. After three months you are led away to a wall in a garden where you are shot by firing squad. Your last memory is the sound of birds chirping their morning calls, then rudely interrupted by the crack of gunfire.

You have failed. You just didn't have enough time. Goto 001 to try again.

377

You are in luck, no one seems to be coming. You turn back and look at the kitchen wondering if there is anything of help here. You may not have much time. Do you,

Search the larder – **076**

Check the cupboards – **036**

Examine the work surfaces – **056**

Leave and go back to the landing – **016**

378

You say in English, in the quietest whisper, that you are here to help. The old woman gives a gentle nod indicating she has understood. The sweat on your brow is swept away by your hand but you know it's more than the hot day causing it. Saying only that she should follow you, you slowly direct your charge to the main street where you know your resistance colleagues will be waiting. They have a car in place to sweep you both away if you give the nod. But although that's the fastest way out of here, it may look a little out of place and arouse suspicion. There's a horse and cart with a resistance fighter at the reins on the far side of the road or you could also walk out of town back to your farm. This would leave you exposed for a long time but may also be the most natural way to route.

Do you,

Wave over to the car and speed away to safety – **388**

Make your way to the horse and cart and leave town that way – **109**

Walk out of town on foot back to the farmhouse – **408**

379

You arrive at the staircase and see a guard is in your way. The guard stands at the bottom of a wooden staircase that has an ornate carpet beginning from the floor but seemingly running up the stairs. At least your journey up will be quiet. The rest of the space at the foot of the stairs is lit by a few lamps but is rather gloomy.

You will need to get past this guard if you are to have access to the rooms above but it is the middle of the night and you will need a good excuse. You haven't got anything around you that would help, so you desperately search the space around the staircase with your eyes. What story will you come up with? Do you,

Take your papers out and hold them as you pass the guard, pretending they are documents for the General – **219**

Tell the guard that the General requires you for some urgent typing – **299**

Tell the guard that you need access to the documents upstairs – **319**

Tell the guard that you have spoken to the desk soldier already – **399**

380

Opening the cabinet you find another key inside. This one has green markings on it and you pocket it swiftly before closing the key cabinet.

Return to **290** and choose another option

381

You hold your breath and watch as the first guard walks past you, his head out to sea. But the next guard looks straight at you, his eyes becoming alive as he sees you huddled behind the barricade. He points a gun at you, shouting at you to stand in German. You stay down, pretending to not know German but then he hauls you to your feet. They take you away to a cell where you have to explain yourself over the coming week. But they don't believe you and you are treated as a spy, one who never sees the end of the war or her homeland again. Still at least you didn't know anything so you had nothing to tell them.

You failed. Goto 001 to start again but remember the real spies never got to start over.

382

You arrive at the bridge and see that there are a number of German positions around it. In order to blow it up, you will need to approach by river quietly and then climb under the structure to plant your explosives and attach your detonators. This will take time but you could just try a less involved method of planting the explosives but it may not be as effective. If you try the more involved method you will only have a few operatives in town to steal your Gestapo car and to follow the prisoner. If you use the less involved method you can send more people. Which will you do? Do you,

Send only a few people and make sure you secure the explosives in the best possible way – **402**

Risk setting the explosives in a less involved fashion and send a larger team to the town – **422**

383

You take out the key and open the door of the cell. The airman steps forward smiling and shakes you by the hand.

Goto **423**

384

You decide whilst in the grounds you would be better served in the outrider's disguise and make your way directly to the chateau. As you approach, a senior German officer passes by and you salute him. He salutes back and walks on allowing you to move on as well. You see the kitchen door before you. This may be a good option as you would avoid any interest from the guard on the front door. However, the front door is also only a short walk away. Do you,

Enter via the kitchen door – **484**

Route and enter via the front door – **447**

385

You take your shoes off and leave them at the top of the stairs. Carefully, you pick your way down the wooden outside of each step and come gradually closer to the guard. You hear him breathe deeply, almost sigh and freeze right behind him. But he doesn't move and you continue your approach. With a quick hand, you reach round and hold the chloroform over his mouth and nose. He struggles and you have to hang on tight for a moment until the chloroform kicks in and he drops like a stone.

You catch him and hold his weight, setting him down gently so as not to alert anyone. He is heavy to drag and so you just get moving. You decide that it would be best to go out the way you came in as you know what to expect. Did you,

Enter via the kitchen initially - **058**

Enter via the front entrance - **078**

386

The man pulls away from you in surprise and demands to know, in French, what you are doing? You hope that the Gestapo officer doesn't speak French as you tell the man he is a fool and the enemy is all around you, and you require his help. But the Gestapo officer seems to speak enough French as he takes you by the arm and asks you in French, why you think he is the enemy.

You are taken away to a van outside the station and blindfolded before going on a journey that ends in a cell. You never return home to England, one of the many who give their lives in the war.

You have failed. Maybe next time you won't rely on chance. Of course in real life they never got a second go. But you can by going to 001.

387

You apologise to the chef and walk away quietly to the back door and step outside. You hide in the shadows and watch the door for twenty minutes. Everything seems to have stayed quiet and so you decide you need to get back into the chateau. Do you,

Re-enter the kitchen – **427**

Go to the front entrance and try to get in there – **447**

388

Standing on one side of the main street, you wave over at the car and it turns across the road before parking up with you. You gently help the old woman into the car and then get into the other side yourself. The car pulls away but you can already hear cries in the street. The sound of motorcycles accompanies these cries and your driver puts down the accelerator hoping to get out of town quick.

You find yourself flung this way and that as a cat and mouse chase begins around the town until you turn a corner and see a line of soldiers and cars blocking the road. In the hail of bullets that follow you, you receive a fatal injury and turn to see the face of your new arrival, quiet and eyes closed. Then there's just the noise of soldiers opening the door before everything is gone.

You have failed. Not smart taking a car when you clearly are not a person to use one regularly. Try again at 001.

389

The British airman says he will create a diversion for you to get away and leaves you before you can say any different. This should give you a chance. You had thought about things you could use in the storeroom but because your friend has run off you need to be ready to take advantage of his diversion.

You wait at the back door until you hear shouts and screams coming from a short distance away. You see Germans running towards the sound and you take the chance to help the prisoner outside. At the front of the building you see a laundry van and you both get into the front seats. There's no keys in the ignition but you fiddle with the wires and jump start it. The vehicle is moving and now you need to decide where to go to complete your escape.

The east gate – **269**

The west gate – **429**

The north gate – **309**

390

You approach the key cabinet and notice that it has strong lock and that you are unlikely to smash open the small cabinet. However you may be able to open it with something that can pick the lock or with an appropriate key. (*Deduct 1 min from your time for this examination*) Do you,

Try a key you have – **410**

Use a hairpin – **430**

Otherwise return to **290** and choose another option

Or has time gone for you, in which case – **376**

391

You take exception to his wanting the plans and turn away telling him no. Suddenly there's a gunshot from the other man on the bridge. He has shot the man you were talking to and is shouting at you to run his way. It dawns on you, you have been talking to a German spy and you run as fast as you can.

Did you injure your leg in a fall from a train – **411**

If not – **431**

392

You carry the prisoner through to the kitchen and strip the Chef, dressing the prisoner in the white jacket and stripy trousers. It's not the best disguise but at least it's something. Go back to **332** and read on below where you left off.

393

The wardrobe is rather ornate and seems to hold several uniforms of the General. There are a lot of uniforms to search through and you will need to check the interior of the furniture for secret compartments. You estimate this could take you about 3 mins. You have already spent a minute searching this far. (*Deduct 1 min now from your time.*) Do you,

Continue with a thorough search of the wardrobe – **413**

Give up searching this item. If so, return to **213** and chose another action

Or has time gone for you, in which case – **376**

394

Everything seems to be quite calm and controlled so you decide to sit and wait it out. You watch the guard speak to his colleagues and three of them come out and begin to shut the large gate. You ask the guard what is the matter and he tells you they are on lock down due to the intruder, no one comes or goes. And that means you are now trapped inside while they check everyone's papers and stories in detail.

Inevitably they discover who you are when they search you. You are taken to a nearby prison for questioning and torture over the next three weeks. Then a bright morning dawns and you are escorted by a squad of soldiers to a wall where their commanding officer instructs them to shoot you. You die in a foreign field like so many heroes.

You have failed. Sometimes you just have to seize the bull by the horns. Try again at 001.

395

It's asking a lot of yourself to smash a drawer open but you think you can do it. However it won't be easy and will take 5 minutes for each drawer to be broken open. There are three drawers, top, middle and bottom. Each time you smash one open, take 5 minutes off your time. This includes your search time for inside the drawer. Goto **415**

396

The guard from downstairs suddenly comes back and says that you have been here a long time and he wonders why you are not finished. He has a much dimmer view of what you are at. Pointing his gun at you he asks you to come with him. He takes you at gunpoint to the front of the building where he finds additional guards.

You are covered with a hood and find yourself next in a cell. For days you are questioned and tortured, giving up many secrets. After three months you are led away to a wall in a garden where you are shot by firing squad. Your last memory is the sound of birds chirping their morning calls, then rudely interrupted by the crack of gunfire.

You have failed. You just didn't have enough time. Goto 001 to try again.

397

You look out to the hall and there are voices coming. There's no way out of this room and you run to hide in the larder. Within a minute the room is flooded with Germans and they take no time in finding you and the British airman. You are both escorted downstairs and thrown into a van where you have a bag placed over your head.

The next thing you see is the inside of a cell after a journey in a vehicle. This turns out to be your home for the next three months as you are interrogated.

Every day there are questions and pain until one bright morning you are led to a wall in a field and face a squad of German soldiers. This is where your war ends, another hero lost in a foreign field.

You have failed. Bringing an extra prisoner with you was a little off mission. Try again at 001.

398

Something in your gut says this isn't right and waving your apology with your hands, you leave the old woman. You spend the rest of the day looking around for your new arrival but every meeting draws a blank. Sitting in the farmhouse that night you receive a message from a resistance runner who says that the arrival was captured in town, dressed as an old woman. You realise your mistake. Sometimes you need to take a risk but knowing when, is a difficult thing to do. There's nothing for it but to continue the work but if you get through the war you know that this bad decision cost someone their life.

Goto **003**

399

You tell the guard that you have already spoken to the desk soldier about why you are here and he gave you permission to go upstairs. The soldier is abrupt saying the decision on who goes upstairs is entirely his but if you wait there he will talk to the desk soldier. As he walks off to the front entrance, you watch him closely and see that he seems fairly happy and even laughs at one point with the other soldier. On return he indicates you can go upstairs. You thank him and begin to climb the stairs.

You are about to climb the stairs but at this point mark down in the notes section at the back of the book that you have 45 mins of time to operate before the guard will become suspicious. In the following passages you will be advised when to deduct time and what to do if time runs out.

Good luck and goto **419**

400

You smile at the Germans and although they seem concerned they keep their distance. You wander along until you spot a laundry van in front of the building. You both get in and find the keys missing from the ignition. Luckily you manage to jump start it and get the vehicle moving. Now how do you get clear from the compound? Which gate will you head for?

The east gate – **269**

The west gate – **429**

The north gate – **309**

401

In the hay barn, your new guide runs through all you need to know about your new cover for the next part of your journey. You are to board a train at a nearby village. At an unknown station, you will be hailed by another resistance member who will join you on the train for two stops before disembarking with you and taking you to your next hiding place.

He hands you an American passport and tells you, you are now Amy Jones, a reporter with the New York Times. This is a great cover as you lived in New York and you know the Times will back up any telephone calls about you. Currently you are on assignment to find out about the situation in occupied France and to send back weekly reports from the area. As such you will be based in a fairly large town but you won't know which until you arrive. If asked you are to state you are connecting through at Lyon.

The man also has a change of clothes for you, all in your size, and all brightly coloured. You certainly will stand out somewhat in a lot of the clothing but as a reporter that is part of your cover, for you are an affluent American in this recently impoverished part of the world. You are also advised to flirt with the Germans when you can, to help disguise your loathing of what they are doing to Europe. At least you get to use your real accent.

He tells you to get a decent night's sleep as you will move out tomorrow, arriving in a car at the station. The night is quiet on the farm but you hear the occasional aeroplane pass overhead and your nerves keep you awake for at least half the night. In the morning you wash in a basin of cold water, apply a little of the perfume in your bag and spruce yourself up.

At nine o'clock a car pulls up outside the barn and you are ushered into it by your guide. He tells you that all plans are set and that once you are dropped at the station you are on your own until the contact boards the train. He says that the contact will mention the city "Philadelphia" during the conversation with you and if no one says this before you arrive at your destination in Lyon, you are to find the Cafe Jardin, order a coffee and wait.

You nod your understanding and try to sit back relaxed in the car. Your guide shakes your hand and wishes you "Bonne chance" and then gets out of the car, disappearing behind a nearby street corner. As the car drives along country roads, you think through all you have to do, practising your smile for any would-be accusers.

The car pulls up at a country station where there are only two other people waiting for the train. Your driver drops your bag at your feet on the station and then leaves once you have tipped him some francs. And then you sit on the bench at the station awaiting the train. It arrives in a blanket of steam and you search out the premiere class, taking your seat in a compartment that contains a German officer.

He wears the uniform of the regular German Army and you can see he is a Captain. You flash a smile at him and he looks back, admiring you and making it obvious he likes your style. He leans forward and asks your name and you answer "Amy". He tells you his and you simply refer to him as Captain before telling him about your trip from America via Britain. He is interested in the American's view of the war and you chat politely about opinions back in the States. He offers you a cigarette and although you don't smoke you take one anyway and let him light it for you.

The train passes through the countryside before arriving at a town where the station has three lines running through it. As you look out the window you see the dark uniform of the Gestapo, and you try not to flinch at the sight but instead look interested. A face then appears at the window of the cabin you are seated in. It has a black cap on its head and a black uniform. It appears the Gestapo are searching the train and you will have to deal with them face to face. Will your papers and cover story be good enough? Or can you avoid the confrontation?

Do you –

Leave the train as fast as you can - **421**

Continue to chat to the German soldier - **441**

Make excuses and make your way to the train toilet - **087**

402

The penetration of the bridge interior is a long job as you quietly work your way up the riverbank and then silently begin to hang underneath the bridge. Working in the dark without any lights is not easy but you have trained for this and it feels good to bring all that training into use. You work steadily, covered by the team around you, protecting your back with calls when patrols are near and assisting with getting the explosives into the difficult positions.

As you are finishing, you hear a bird call indicating that the train is approaching. Quickly you get off the underside of the bridge but are unable to get to the detonators. But by having so many people around you are able to trust them to set off the explosives and as you rush to get clear you hear the deafening sound and feel the rush of wind and heat past your head. Lying in the grass you see the iron structure collapse and the train plummets off the bridge into the water.

You retreat with your team and head for the farmhouse to await word from the small team who went to the town to try and steal a Gestapo vehicle to follow the prisoner. Around dawn they arrive back to cheers from the team. They managed to track the prisoner to a barracks but who knows how long he will be there.

You and your team go to bed while others from the resistance set about gathering plans and documents about this new location. As you sleep, the local Frenchmen and women risk their lives so that when you wake up you will have the chance to infiltrate the barracks and rescue the prisoner. Open your eyes at **004.**

403

You take out one of the small vials and crack it open over the top of the lock. It runs down into the latch mechanism, dissolving away the metal. Soon you are able to force the door of the cell and the airman steps out smiling. He shakes you by the hand, ready to assist.

Goto **423**

404

You drive the sidecar up to the hardstanding and try to spy out a parking spot beside the array of classy vehicles. Every car of the seven parked on the hardstanding looks immaculate and seems to be a staff car for dignitaries. You can see a lot of spare hardstanding available. The access to the chateau from here is perfect, less than twenty seconds walk. Do you,

Select a spot and park the sidecar – **424**

Decide that the other areas might be better – **444**

405

You risk stepping down the outside of the stairs and cringe with every loud step you make. It doesn't take long for the guard to turn around and ask what you are doing walking down the outside of the stairs, ruining the wood. You can tell his suspicions are aroused and he watches your hands carefully. He must have caught a glimpse of the cloth because he raises his gun and asks you to show what's in your hands.

Other guards are called and soon you are lead outside to a van where a black cloth is placed over your head. You wake up in a cell and from there you suffer three months of questioning and torture. Then on a sunny, crisp morning you are led away to a small wall, accompanied by six soldiers and an officer. There you are shot by firing squad, another hero who falls on a foreign shore.

You have failed. Not a very subtle spy. Try again at 001.

406

You call out in French to hang on as you are getting dressed. There comes another knock telling you to open up right away. You open the door slightly and shove your papers through the gap, saying you will be opening the door fully in a moment. Your papers are whipped away and you open the door a few moments later.

The Gestapo officer looks at you quizzically and you wonder if the sweat you feel running between your shoulder blades is matched by any on your forehead. The man shows no emotion as he reads your passport and then asks where you come from in America. New York, you say flicking your hair back, giving a proud air.

The officer turns to colleague and spits out the word "American". It appears he doesn't like people from over the water but he hands your papers back to you, nodding curtly and then leaving you to return to your

seat. You concentrate hard so your hands don't shake
as you resume your seat in the cabin and smile at the
German army captain. You cannot help but feel that
was a close one. However you are now continuing your
journey, watching the fields roll past as the train puffs
along.

Goto – **206**

407

You calmly take off your outriders cap and jacket,
telling him that you are a female auxiliary on your way
for a quiet rendezvous with the General. You say that
the General doesn't want anyone to know about the
pair of you so the chef had better stay quiet. In fact he
can store your disguise for you in the cupboards.

He has a look of amazement but he seems to be
swallowing your story completely. You tell him to go
back to sleep after he stores your clothing and you will
say no more about it to anyone. It's probably best the
General doesn't know that he knows about their secret
liaison. The chef nods.

You walk out of the storeroom in your auxiliary
uniform and make for the hallway beyond.

Goto **200**

408

Holding the old woman's arm, you slowly walk along the main street heading back to the road that will lead out of town and back to your farmhouse base. You feel the stares of people looking at you and this hobbling dear, and you wonder if your pretence is good enough. Your colleague grabs your arm at one point and you fear they have seen something but it's only part of the act. They simply wanted to make a stop for breath.

As you reach the edge of the town, you see a check point full of German guards. They seem to be checking everyone's papers and after last night's debacle with the parachute drop you suspect this is a routine precaution against any enemy who may have arrived.

You are at the back of the small line waiting to have their papers examined and you have a sudden thought. Does your new arrival have papers for their current disguise? Will they pass through alright or will they be arrested and you with them? Maybe there is another option. You could run. It would be a serious risk but you might be able to get into an alley and escape out of town by another route. Or you could leave the line quietly and take up a hiding spot if followed.

Leaving the line will cause suspicion and will most definitely result in being tailed in the current climate. But it will provoke less of a response than simply running.

You look at your new arrival. They are disguised as an old woman but just how fast and fit are they underneath that costume? It's hard to tell as the body is so well covered by the black mourning outfit they wear. But the line is moving and you need to make a decision. Do you,

Run as fast as you can from the line – **428**

Wait in line and trust your papers – **448**

Leave the line and slowly make your way back into town – **468**

409

You remember the German you knocked out in the store and realise you could dress the prisoner up in those clothes and try to find a vehicle and then try to make a run for it. The prisoner will be slow but at least he wouldn't be so obvious.

If this sounds like a plan – **449**

If not then reassess what you want to do at **312**

410

Is your key from the ring of keys in the kitchen – **450**

Is your key yellow or blue marked – **470**

411

You try to run quickly but your leg is holding you back. You hear another gunshot and realise this one has hit you. Falling to the ground you clutch the plans but soon your eyes close for good.

You have failed. So close yet so far. Try again at 001.

412

You carry the prisoner through to the kitchen and begin to exchange his clothes for the chef's clothes, who is still lying on the floor. Halfway through changing him, you hear a voice at the door. It's the Commandant who has returned to his office and found it empty. On searching he has found you in the kitchen. Calling for some guards, he has you taken away and placed in a van downstairs with a bag over your head.

After a short journey, you are deposited into a cell and the bag removed. This turns out to be your home for the next three months as you are interrogated. Every day there are questions and pain until one bright morning you are led to a wall in a field and face a squad of German soldiers. This is where your war ends, another hero lost in a foreign field.

You have failed. Always remember to keep an eye on the clock! Try again at 001.

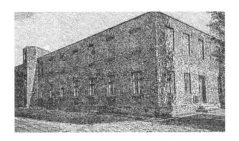

413

You look through all the pockets and interior of the General's suits, even under the epaulettes on the shoulders where you can but you find nothing. A hand search of the interior and exterior of the wardrobe can find nothing out of the ordinary. This appears to be just a wardrobe with clothes in it. (*Deduct 3 mins from your time.*)

Return to **213** and choose another option

Or has time gone for you, in which case – **376**

414

You sense something is wrong and open the throttle on the sidecar and smash through the barrier out onto the open road beyond. By the reaction of the guards, you may have made the right decision.

Behind, you hear cries and shouts to follow that sidecar but you don't care and have raced away to a side road within five minutes to find a car waiting there with the keys in it. The resistance have come through again. You now face the trek back to England but at least you are clear of the chateau with a fighting chance. Goto **434**

415

Do you want to smash open the,

Top drawer – **435**

Middle drawer – **455**

Bottom drawer – **475**

Or do you just want to go back and search another part of the room – **275**

416

You enter the General's office and see a large desk in the middle of the room. It has a number of drawers either side of the seat, all of which have keyholes, indicating they might be locked. On the far side of the room is a small wardrobe and a drinks cabinet beside it. There's also a blacked out window and a safe in the far corner of the room.

The room has a feeling of grandeur and there's a portrait of the Führer on the wall. Obviously a working room, its secrets seem to be stored away at this time. (*If this is your first time in this room, your quick look around has cost you 1 min of time.*) Do you,

Examine the drawers of the desk – **436**

Check out the wardrobe – **094**

Look at the drinks cabinet – **114**

Look beyond the window – **134**

Examine the safe – **029**

Or do you wish to leave the room and instead

Look around the landing for any help – **439**

Try the door that says "Meeting Room" - **077**

Try the door that says "Communications Room – **216**

Try the unmarked door – **356**

Or has time gone for you, in which case – **376**

417

The chef sees the British airman in his German outfit and immediately stands up straight. The chef announces that lunch will be ready within the hour. The British airman says nothing, and actually seems a little confused. He strolls over to the chef who is looking at you both and his mind seems to be coming to the idea that you are not who you say you are.

The airman has spotted this though and knocks the chef out with a punch to the jaw. Carefully he pulls him behind a table so he cannot be seen from the doorway. You may not have much time to search the kitchen for anything useful. Do you,

Search the larder - **076**

Check the cupboards - **036**

Examine the work surfaces - **056**

Leave and go back to the landing - **016**

418

You approach the peasant man lying in the grass looking at the river meander its way past him. He seems to be enjoying the sun and relaxing. He looks up at you as you approach and simply smiles announcing that it is a beautiful day in French. You point to your mouth indicating that you cannot speak and he nods his head. He laughs a little and says you will be the perfect companion, as he hates too much noise.

You try to engage him but it is hard work. Waving your hands you try to ask where he is from but he struggles to comprehend. You seem to be getting nowhere with this man and you are none the wiser as to whether he is the new arrival you are looking for. Do you,

Speak openly to him in a hushed whisper – **438**

Continue in silence to see if he proffers anything more – **458**

Leave the peasant man and if you haven't already,

Talk to the old woman -**358**

Talk to the German soldier -**298**

Talk to the Beggar – **009**

419

You climb the stairs which are in reasonable darkness, only a few dim lights illuminating the staircase. On the walls you can see paintings and other fine furnishings of a rich French past. But you try to keep a focus on where you are going and arrive at a landing off of which run several rooms.

There is a sign that says "General's Office" on a door which is shut, a sign that says "Meeting Room", another door that says "Communications Room" and a door which has no sign. Apart from these doors there is just the landing you are currently standing on. Time is ticking and you need to get on with your mission. Do you,

Look around the landing for any help - **439**

Try the door that says "General's Office" - **479**

Try the door that says "Meeting Room" - **077**

Try the door that says "Communications Room - **216**

Try the unmarked door - **356**

420

The day is still warm and you walk round town with the old woman, occasionally stopping at a bench or a wall. Every time you circle round you see the roadblock is still there. And there is also the question of the man in the suit, who still seems to be following you. But you have made the decision and surely they will not keep the roadblock up all night.

With the light fading you see the soldiers beginning to stand down and leave the roadside, allowing free passage out of the town. You take the old woman's hand and together you walk slowly out, breathing in the cool air now coming to the world in the absence of sunlight.

As you walk along the road in the dark, a car pulls up and you are bundled into it by some rough men. Inside the car is the gentleman who had been watching you through the day. He gives his apologies but he thought a daylight grab would attract suspicion. He doesn't say another word and the car drives moderately along the road until you reach the farmhouse where you are based.

You are dropped off and you thank the men who are presumably from the resistance. Once inside the farmhouse, the farmhouse owner tells you she thought it prudent to have a backup plan and you thank her for it.

She takes the old woman through to the barn and up into the loft where you have your radio equipment. There the old woman undresses and changes into a smart pair of trousers and blouse, ready for her next journey. She's a brunette, young, and very smart looking, completely different from the disguise she had employed up to this stage. You don't ask her name but you do bid her a fond farewell that night when the car comes to take her away.

You may not have known her name, or even where she comes from, but this is a small win in the war and you celebrate that in your head. Life returns back to normal, monitoring communications and passing messages but another mission will not be that far away.

Find out what it is at **003**

421

You panic and push your way out of the cabin onto the platform. Looking around, you see stairs leading down and underneath the track. You try to run as fast as you can in your heels but Gestapo officers move in from all sides. You are taken to the back of a truck and from there to a prison cell. Held as a spy, your days are filled with questions and pain before you end the war, buried in a foreign field.

You have failed. Panic is not something a spy can afford. Start over again at 001.

422

Being worried about obtaining a Gestapo car, you send the bulk of your team to the town to achieve this objective. This leaves you very few people to set up the explosives with the amount of Germans about. You route along the riverbank and quickly set up the explosives although you have reduced the target of your explosions to four support pillars. If you are honest, you are unsure if you have done enough and you believe there will be an element of luck to this.

You sit by the detonators as the train approaches and you set off the explosives in good time. You hear the screech of the train brakes and watch nervously as the supports you targeted shake. Have you done enough? I guess it's in the lap of the gods.

Try **442**

Or try **462**

423

"So do you want me to stick around and assist, or shall I cause a diversion of some sort?" The airman makes a compelling offer as a diversion might take any heat off of you. But at the moment you are also undiscovered and the barracks has no idea they are being infiltrated. This could be a key decision. Also, you may be sending him to his doom by asking him to create a diversion as it is unlikely he is going to survive on his own amongst foreign forces in his uniform. Do you,

Ask him to go and cause a diversion – **443**

Tell him to stick with you – **463**

424

You find a clear spot and park up the sidecar. A German soldier runs up to you and asks in German what you are doing. You tell him you are parking up and are going to the chateau. He tells you that you cannot park here and was it not obvious from the other cars in the area. You apologise and say it is your first time here. He shakes his head and says that the men on the gate would have told you to park in the barn.

Suddenly he is pointing his weapon at you and asking you to accompany him. You are taken towards the front door of the chateau where he tells other soldiers what has happened and to get a Captain. When asked by the senior officer what you are doing here, you reply you are delivering a message but it's too secret for you to divulge who to. He makes a quick call to someone and on his return he orders you to be taken away to be interrogated. The drive to a prison is not long and is done with a hood over your head.

A month later, having extracted all the information from you they can, the Germans take you outside on a clear morning and line you up before a firing squad. Your mission ends as another fallen hero on distant shores.

You have failed. You were told where to park! Try again at 001.

425

You creep down the centre of the stairs utilising the carpet to keep your movements quiet. It goes well until you get to the last step and you are a few feet from the guard. As you step across to him he begins to turn and you fling yourself at him. You don't have a proper grip on him but you do have the cloth at his mouth. But can you hold it there? Just how strong is this guard? At the moment your decision seems to be resting on a good deal of luck. Find out how lucky you are,

Go Here – **445**

Or go here – **465**

426

You push back some luggage and shout out your position. In your hand you hold out your papers. These are taken but you are frog marched from the train into a waiting van and driven at speed to a prison. There you remain in a cell for three months only being allowed out to be tortured and questioned. You never leave that prison, another war casualty who never made it home.

You have failed. If you wish to start again goto 001.

427

You re-enter the kitchen and as you walk in the chef emerges from the larder seeing you again. He shouts for the guard and although you turn and bolt out of the door, you are caught in open ground and hear the gunfire that signals your doom. You end your mission lying on the grass of the chateau in the middle of the night.

You have failed. Maybe a new path would help. Goto 001 to try again.

428

You grab your colleague's hand and tell them to run now as hard and as fast as they can. Together the two of you race off back up the main street. You hear soldiers shouting and then more soldiers emerge from up ahead, from out of alleys and doorways. You panic and cut across the street in front of carts and small cars but your new arrival doesn't follow and you hear gunfire.

Something hits the ground behind you but you don't look back, simply running for the nearest alleyway, trying to get some sort of protection. But something hits your back making you tumble to the ground. There's further gunfire but everything is fading and then suddenly there is no more.

You have failed. But you can try again at 001.

429

As you drive up to the west gate you realise that you are in luck as there are only a small amount of Germans here. They are stopping vehicles but you wait until they are all occupied and then drive hard towards the gate. By the time they have reacted you have smashed through the gate and are heading along the road. The pursuit is slow in coming and you are able to turn into a side road where a car pulls up alongside you.

You get out of the van and get your prisoner from the rear, and together you get into the resistance car and speed off. You are dropped off behind your farmhouse base and you wave goodbye to the prisoner and airman who the resistance will now move on.

Telling London that night on the radio of a successful mission is a joy but you know you will not have to wait long before the next mission arrives.

Goto **005**

430

You take out the hairpin you found in the General's bathroom and try to pick the lock. It's a sturdy lock but you manage to pick it eventually. (*Deduct 4 mins for this effort.*)

Goto **380**

Or has time gone for you, in which case – **396**

431

You run as hard as you can but hear another gunshot. You have been hit on the shoulder but you keep going and round the corner of the bridge past the first man. You see a dinghy and two men waving at you. Diving into the water you are soon pulled on board and the dingy heads up river and out to sea, covered by the dark of the night.

Goto **489**

432

You remember that the storeroom had Jerry cans of petrol and that the boiler had a means to ignite them. Leaving the prisoner for a few moments, you race to the store and then start pouring the petrol from them over the boiler in the next room. Opening the front you watch it catch fire and begin to burn quickly. You need to get on the move and fast.

Goto **472**

433

You walk up close to the bed and stare down at a bald headed man who is snoring lightly. He seems to be wearing pyjamas and has something under his pillow. It seems strangely large, about the size of hand, or maybe slightly larger. You cannot tell in the dark. Taking a look would certainly be a risk. (*Deduct 1 min from your total time as you have had to stare for a while to see these things.*) Do you,

Try to take the item from under the pillow – **453**

Leave the General in peace to sleep. If so, return to **213** and choose another option

Or has time gone for you, in which case – **376**

434

You drive the car without lights in the dark until you reach an old cottage where you turn into a barn. As you drive through the doors of the barn, two men pull the doors shut and a woman greets you inside. She takes you inside the cottage and hides you in an upstairs room where you are given a meal to eat. The woman never mentions her name and you see no one else. However you hear the car being driven away, presumably to be abandoned elsewhere as a decoy.

After a few hours rest you are placed into the rear of a lorry taking boxes of apples to market. You are hidden deep within the lorry and are bounced about until it stops. From the noises around you, you can tell you are in a town. When the boxes are removed, you are taken by a young boy through the streets to a watchmaker's shop where you are given a blouse, jacket, tight skirt and high heels. You apply makeup and resume your American journalist disguise.

From there you walk into the train station and catch a train for the coast. Settling in for the journey you try not to appear too precious about the case you have in the luggage rack above you. Inside a secret compartment are the plans you need to get to London. You know you will spend the day on this train and when you reach your destination you will have to find a contact with a small dinghy who will take you out to a British vessel just off the coast. You know this is far from over.

As you step off the train, the station is dimly lit and you can see a large number of German soldiers about the area. Interspersed are Gestapo officers and you get the feeling they know your intentions to come here. But there is nothing to do except execute the plan as you have no back up in this town. It seems you may have to play cat and mouse in this place.

As you walk towards the exit you are stopped by a Gestapo officer who asks for your papers. You hand them over immediately and he scans them thoroughly. Instead of letting you leave he asks where you are going tonight. Do you,

Tell him you are seeking a hotel before travelling on tomorrow – **454**

Tell him you are staying with friends – **112**

Tell him you are going to the nearest bar for a drink as you are exhausted from your travels – **052**

Tell him you are just resting a few hours before your next train out of here - **132**

435

The top drawer reveals a collection of family photos and letters from home in German to the Commandant. There are drawings from his children and a letter of commendation from a senior officer but nothing of use to you.

Goto **415**

436

You kneel down in front of the drawers and see that they are flush with the desk making opening them impossible without using a key. There doesn't seem to be anything else extraordinary about them and maybe you have a key that fits. (*This examination has cost you 1 min.*) Do you,

Try a key or a hairpin – **456**

Look elsewhere in the room. In which case return to **416** and choose another option.

Or has time gone for you, in which case – **376**

437

The chef replies to you in German asking why you are here. As you tell him you are here to assist in the kitchen he comes close to you, saying that he has never heard any of the French maids speak so fluently in German. Without warning he grabs your arm and twists it behind your back.

You are escorted downstairs and, after being given to the guards, you are thrown into a van where you have a bag placed over your head.

The next thing you see is the inside of a cell after a journey in a vehicle. This turns out to be your home for the next three months as you are interrogated. Every day there are questions and pain until one bright morning you are led to a wall in a field and face a squad of German soldiers. This is where your war ends, another hero lost in a foreign field.

You have failed. Language is so important. Try again at 001.

438

You tell the man in a hushed whisper that he is with a friend. He seems somewhat panicked and starts to get up to walk away. Do you,

Try to get him to stay – **220**

Let him leave – **478**

439

The landing is dark and you take a look behind the flower pots and the paintings on the wall but you find nothing. You are about to give up when you notice that there is something under the rug that sits in the middle of the landing. It might be nothing but it will take a good few minutes to undo the rug edging where it is fixed down. You have already spent 2 mins searching. (*Take 2 mins off your time left.*) Do you,

Try to look under the carpet at whatever is under the rug – **459**

Or give up looking around the landing and

Try the door that says "General's Office" – **479**

Try the door that says "Meeting Room" - **077**

Try the door that says "Communications Room – **216**

Try the unmarked door – **356**

Or has time gone for you, in which case – **376**

440

You say that you are just in to make an early start on the day's typing. The soldier seems unconvinced and shouts over to the woman on the switchboard to ask if she has seen you before. She shakes her head and he then takes a closer look at your papers. After a minute he asks the telephone operator to contact the officer in charge of the auxiliaries to confirm who you are.

You know you are rumbled and turn and run out the front door. As you make for the perimeter to try and head out to open countryside, a jeep pulls up and you are shot trying to climb a wall. Your last breath is in the chateau grounds, hearing the boots of your shooter approaching you.

You have failed. You need a better cover story. Goto 001 to try again.

441

You realise that the rapport you have built up with the German Captain could be useful and you ask if he minds if you sit beside him. He accepts and you ask him about his heroic deeds in the war while looking deep into his eyes. You can tell he is falling for your charms and he becomes indignant when the Gestapo enter the cabin, demanding why they are interrupting him.

Despite his protests, the Gestapo officer insists on seeing your documents, insisting that Americans would not be on this train. Is this situation becoming dangerous or are you still in control? Do you,

Decide this is all too close for comfort and make a run for it – **421**

Continue with your cover as an American reporter – **461**

Ask for a moment with the German Captain - **127**

442

You watch in disbelief as the supports don't crumble but instead look to be as strong as ever as the train reaches the bridge. Going slowly, it crosses over and you find yourself having to run for cover as the countryside is swarmed with Germans.

You get clear but you failed to stop this major coup for the Germans and find that the information taken from the prisoner in Germany creates a decisive moment in the war.

You have failed. A job's not worth doing unless you do it right! Try again at 001.

443

You tell him that the prisoner you seek is of prime importance and that any diversion he could offer would be most welcome. He nods and thinks for a moment. Give me ten minutes to get elsewhere he says. If you have a German uniform, you give it to him to wear. Wishing you the best of British luck, he disappears out of the cells. You admire his bravery as you have basically asked him to give up his life for the prisoner upstairs. But you cannot hang about either. You decide to leave the cells and look elsewhere. Do you,

If you haven't already, enter the room marked "Boiler" – **028**

Retreat back to the stairs and climb them – **144**

Retreat back to the front corridor if you have not been that way before – **064**

444

As you throttle up again, a soldier runs up towards you and asks what you are doing on the hardstanding. You turn round and profusely apologise saying that you took a wrong turn looking for the barn. He shakes his head and points to the side of the chateau and the green barn that is located there. You give your thanks and drive quickly that direction.

Goto **284**

445

You take a swinging hand from the guard but he only grazes the top of your head and you can hang on, keeping the mouth and nose covered. He quickly collapses and you suck in deep breaths, trying to steady yourself.

You need to move fast and decide to follow the way you came in as your route back out. Did you,

Enter via the kitchen initially – **058**

Enter via the front entrance – **078**

446

You stay silent, hoping and praying that the Gestapo officer will simply move on thinking that this is a stuck toilet cabin. The pounding of the door continues and you suddenly find the door broken off its hinges and falling onto you. Your head takes a nasty bump before you are hauled off the train and placed against a wall. Questions are shouted at you in French and German but you stay quiet. Your papers are taken from you and the Gestapo officer looking at them seems impressed but you over hear them saying, in German, that although things seem to check out, as you were hiding then you must be concealing more.

A man takes you away to a prison cell and days of torture and pain. You never see England but at least they never got any worthwhile information from you. After all, you don't know anything yet.

You have failed. Silence is not always golden. If you want to begin again got 001.

447

You approach the front door of the chateau which is flanked by two marble pillars and sets off the grandeur of this old French building. Inside you can see a dimly lit foyer which has a desk to one side with a soldier sat behind it. On the opposite side is a telecommunications desk, complete with switchboard and a young lady manning it. Both look bored as befits the early morning hours but you have to be on your guard.

A sign says in German that all visitors must report in at the desk and you make your way over to the yawning man behind the desk. He nods at you and you hand over your papers which he barely looks at before asking your business.

You knew this was coming but how do you play this next part? With confidence, or do you act a little shy and pretend you don't know your way? Time to decide. Do you,

Tell the soldier on the desk that you are reporting for duty – **467**

Ask if you are in the right place for the female auxiliaries – **040**

Tell the desk soldier that you have been requested by the General – **100**

Tell the desk soldier that you have work upstairs to complete and need to get it done before the General rises – **160**

448

You decide that trusting in your papers is the best course of action and you believe that if your colleague had a problem with papers they would be telling you now. As the soldiers approach, asking you for papers, you take them out and hand them over. When they start asking questions, you make hand motions to show you are mute but the old woman intervenes speaking out in a perfect French accent, highlighting your condition and then delivering her own papers. Within minutes you are walking on beyond the checkpoint. One of the German soldiers even smiles at you helping this old woman.

Slowly you progress out of town, seeing the traffic pass you both by, an array of horses and carts taking produce, the occasional German outrider or car, and then local peasants making their way back from town. The sun is shining brightly and you are sweating from its heat but also from the near escape you have had.

You feel relieved when you turn into the farmyard where you live and your boss comes out to help the old woman inside. She takes her through to the barn and up into the loft where you have your radio equipment. There the old woman undresses and changes into a smart pair of trousers and blouse, ready for her next journey. She's a brunette, young, and very smart looking, completely different from the disguise she had employed up to this stage. You don't ask her name but you do bid her a fond farewell that night when the car comes to take her away.

You may not have known her name, or even where she comes from, but this is a small win in the war and you celebrate that in your head. Life returns back to normal, monitoring communications and passing messages but another mission will not be that far away.

Find out what it is at **003**

449

You walk out of the building propping up the prisoner in the German uniform. As you hobble along some of the Germans look at you but just how interested are they in you and how good is your disguise?

Maybe it's this good – **469**

Or maybe this good – **400**

Pick one!

450

You try the keys from the ring of keys you found in the kitchen and after a few attempts, one opens the lock easily. (*Deduct 2 mins for this effort.*) Goto **380**

Or has time gone for you, in which case – **396**

451

You decide to skirt past the bridge and route to the riverbank. As you approach it in the dark you can see two men in a dinghy waving at you to enter the water and come to them. They could be anyone but you know you were to meet a dinghy. Do you,

Swim out to the dinghy – **471**

Leave the riverbank instead and,

Approach the first man on the bridge – **291**

Approach the second man on the bridge – **351**

452

The British airman turns to you with a heroic look on his face. He tells you that he will run off and create a distraction allowing you to make a bid for freedom and hopefully get clear. You are full of admiration for this man and you wish him all the best as he heads off to cause as much trouble as he can. It will probably be the last time you see him.

Goto **472**

453

You carefully place your right arm under the pillow and place your hand on what feels like a handgun. But as you move your hand around it, you realise you are disturbing the General who has awoken. You grab the gun and run out of the door, desperately looking for an exit but the General is shouting for his guards. You get to the bottom of the stairs before a guard brings you down with a rapid volley. You fall, another brave hero lost in a foreign field.

You have failed. Best let sleeping dogs lie. Goto 001 to try again.

454

He nods and hands you back your papers but you have the feeling that it was all too easy. As you walk from the train station, you realise you are being followed and by cutting through different side streets you identify at least three men tailing you at different times. There is no way you can simply meet your contact, who should be near a bridge in the town, with this amount of heat following you. You need an alternative plan. Do you,

Book into a hotel - **474**

Drop your case once you have removed the plans, hoping they will drop off you – **032**

Enter a bar – **052**

455

The middle drawer reveals a code book with an encryption key. There are a number of codes in here and each is identified by a two letter symbol. This may be helpful if you have a code to break.

Goto **415**

456

Do you have the keys from the kitchen – **476**

Do you have a hairpin – **280**

Do you have other keys – **074**

457

Do you have a British airman with you? If so – **477**

If not – **260**

458

You sit in silence and so does the peasant man. He seems to simply want to enjoy the river and the sun. Do you,

Speak openly to him in a hushed whisper – **438**

Leave the peasant man and if you haven't already,

Talk to the old woman -**358**

Talk to the German soldier – **298**

Talk to the Beggar - **009**

459

You work at the fixed edges of the rug and manage to break an area loose. Reaching under with your hand, you find a small pair of pliers. These may become useful, who knows, so you pocket them and replace the rug. (*The process has taken 3 mins so take that off your time remaining.*) Time is a ticking so what will you do now. Do you,

Try the door that says "General's Office" – **479**

Try the door that says "Meeting Room" - **077**

Try the door that says "Communications Room – **216**

Try the unmarked door – **356**

Or has time gone for you, in which case – **376**

460

The soldier comes close to you and you hold your breath as best you can. He pulls away one case after another throwing them aside and you feel the sweat drip into your eyes and sting them. But you don't flinch, your very life depends on it. His hand goes to the side of you and then he simply moves on to another case just across from you.

Only when the duo searching have left the wagon do you let out a sigh of relief. But you are not crazy enough to come out until the train begins to move again. With the train back at full speed and racing though the countryside you return to your cabin, finding the German army captain still there. He immediately smiles at you and you nod back. You journey continues for now.

Goto **206**

461

The Gestapo officer asks for papers from you and you hand them over. He stares at them and then asks what newspaper you work for. You reply "The New York Times" and he spits on the ground, saying that he imagines it is a cesspit for everyone coming into the harbour by the Washington monument.

You know that the monument is in Washington but that you cannot see it from so far away in New York.

Instead you would see the Statue of Liberty in New York. Do you,

Correct the officer and point out that the Statue of Liberty stands at the entrance to the harbour – **481**

Tell him that the Washington Monument is in Washington – **007**

Go along with the officer's answer not wanting to antagonise him – **027**

462

Sitting at the detonators, you watch as the train approaches. You set them off in good time and then watch as the train desperately tries to come to a halt. It sails forward just as the bridge collapses and the front carriage and the engine topple into the gap created.

You retreat with your team and head for the farmhouse to await word from the large team who went to the town to try and steal a Gestapo vehicle to follow the prisoner. Around dawn they arrive back to cheers from everyone else. They managed to track the prisoner to a barracks but who knows how long he will be there.

You and your team go to bed while others from the resistance set about gathering plans and documents about this new location. As you sleep, the local Frenchmen and women risk their lives so that when you wake up you will have the chance to infiltrate the barracks and rescue the prisoner. Open your eyes at **004.**

463

You tell him you'll need help with this rescue and ask him to stick with you. He nods and you see a smile on his face. If you have a German uniform you give it to him to wear as a better disguise. At least he has a fighting chance of escape this way. The airman advises that you get a move on upstairs as they will probably be torturing the prisoner if they have taken him upstairs, or they may be prepping him for transport to another prison. You remember how desperate they were to get the prisoner onto the train and you agree you should hurry up. Checking the corridor you sneak back out of the cells closing the door behind you. There's no time to hang about and you move quietly, but with despatch, to the stairs and climb them.

Goto **144**

464

You take a hard left and steer the sidecar behind an area of trees which you find leads to an orchard. Carefully you manoeuvre the vehicle behind a broken down wall and then find some branches from a nearby tree to hide it. You also take off your outrider's disguise, leaving the clothing in the sidecar and smooth out your auxiliary uniform before finding the small path that leads back to the chateau. The area you are in is quiet and only once do you hear a patrol jeep pass but you take cover in good time.

You walk out of the trees and towards the front door and wonder if this is the best approach. Maybe you could go to the kitchen door at the rear of the chateau and make a less obvious entrance. But then again you are now in a uniform that says you are meant to be here. Do you,

Enter by the front door – **447**

Enter via the kitchen door – **484**

465

You take a swinging hand from the guard and it catches you in the middle of the face. You can't hold onto the cloth and you spin off him. As you turn to get back at the guard, you hear the gunshot and feel the pain of the stomach wound. With another gunshot you feel nothing more, as everything fades to black.

You have failed. Guess you are not so lucky. Try again at 001.

466

You decide to stay hidden. You must believe you are a lucky person. Are these soldiers good, quality searchers? Are they thorough? Time to find out.

Goto **460**

Or goto **013**

467

In your best German you tell the soldier that you are reporting for duty and he looks closely at you. In reply to your statement, he asks what duty you have at this hour of the morning when most of the chateau are asleep. Do you,

Say you are just getting in early to start on the day's typing – **440**

Say with confidence you have some work for the General which needs to be ready by morning – **020**

468

You pull gently on the old woman's arm and start to walk out of the line back into town. You feel the merest resistance as if this is a bad idea but she comes with you. Slowly you make your way along to the bread shop and in the reflection of the window you can see a dapperly dressed man watching you. You are being tailed.

To avoid suspicion, you enter the bread shop and purchase a loaf, hoping that on exit he will have moved on. But he's still there across the street and clearly he is intent on watching you. You need to decide what to do now and quickly. You could return back to the line and take your chances with your papers. Or you could try to leave town by the other end and then circumnavigate round back onto the road to your base. Or you could simply stay in town, waiting for the roadblock on the edge of town to be abandoned. Do you,

Wait in town for the roadblock to be abandoned – **420**

Go back to the line and await the papers check – **448**

Walk out of town by the other end – **033**

469

One of the Germans comes over and asks if the officer is alright. Your prisoner in disguise tries to speak back in German but his speech is slurred and the German investigates further. He soon realises that this is the prisoner and you are held at gunpoint. You are taken away and placed in a van with a bag over your head.

After a short journey, you are deposited into a cell and the bag removed. This turns out to be your home for the next three months as you are interrogated. Every day there are questions and pain until one bright morning you are led to a wall in a field and face a squad of German soldiers. This is where your war ends, another hero lost in a foreign field.

You have failed. Not your lucky day. Try again at 001.

470

You try your key in the lock but it doesn't fit and you are unable to turn the mechanism at all. Despite taking some time over it, nothing budges for you. (*Deduct 2 mins for this effort.*)

Return to **390** and choose another option

Or has time gone for you, in which case – **396**

471

You slowly get into the water and swim out to the dinghy where the men haul you on board. One of the men points to the bridge and indicates to keep quiet, saying one of those men is a German. You give a sigh of relief and sit quietly as the dinghy makes its way out to sea under the cover of darkness.

Goto **489**

472

You look out of the door and wonder what direction to run. You could head for the main gate, to the north. Or you could go to one of the side entrances, to the east or to the west. Do you,

Run north – **360**

Run east – **014**

Run west – **034**

473

Carefully you make your way over to the blacked out windows and sneak a peek behind the curtains and out to the grounds of the chateau. You can see very little except the odd shadow of a patrolling guard. In the 2 minutes that you watch (*Deduct 2 mins from your time*) you see a jeep pass by the front of the house but otherwise nothing of interest.

Return to **213** and choose another option

Or has time gone for you, in which case – **376**

474

You see a small hotel up ahead and enter the lobby. Through the window you can see one of the men who was following you waiting outside. You request a room from the woman behind the desk and she leads you to a second floor room near the bathroom. It's simply furnished and you wonder what your next move is. Do you,

Wait an hour and then leave the room to meet your contact – **320**

Leave now but through the bedroom window at the rear – **012**

475

The bottom drawer contains some medicinal packets and an assortment of creams and lotions. It appears the Commandant is not in the best of health. There is nothing of use here.

Goto **415**

476

You try the keys from the kitchen but nothing seems to work in any of the drawers. (*You spend 3 mins trying all the keys.*)

Do you have other keys or a hairpin to try – **456**

Or has time gone for you, in which case – **376**

If not return to **416** and choose another option

477

You make a rush for the chef with the British airman and together you easily subdue him from behind and use some kitchen tape to tie up his hands and feet and gag his mouth. The airman drags him to a corner of the kitchen that cannot be seen from the landing.

You can now search the kitchen although you'll need to be quick. Do you,

Search the larder – **076**

Check the cupboards – **036**

Examine the work surfaces – **056**

Leave and go back to the landing – **016**

478

The sweat runs down your neck as he leaves. Will he talk to the soldier and tell him what happened or will he simply walk away? As he passes the soldier, your stomach clenches but then becomes less tight as he simply breezes on past. The man seems to have found his peace again and sits down some way along the riverbank. That was simply too close. Do you now,

If you haven't already done so,

Engage the old woman - **358**

Go to the German soldier - **298**

Visit the Beggar - **009**

479

If you have already opened this door - **416**, otherwise

Otherwise the door is locked and will need opening. It has three separate locks each needing a key. Each keyhole has a band around it. One is blue, one green and one yellow. Do you,

Try to force the door - **240**

Go back downstairs and get the guard to open the door – **017**

Do you have keys to try in the locks – **037**

Or do you give up on this door at the moment and instead (*but take 1 min off your time if you choose any of these options*) choose one of the following:

Look around the landing for any help – **439**

Try the door that says "Meeting Room" - **077**

Try the door that says "Communications Room – **216**

Try the unmarked door – **356**

Or has time gone for you, in which case – **376**

480

You take the plans with you into the "Meeting Room" and locate the dumb waiter again. Placing the plans under the dirty crockery, you look for the mechanism to move the plates down and start to operate it.

Did you release the dumb waiter in the kitchen - **018**

If you didn't – **038**

481

"Surely that's enough for you," says the German Captain and the Gestapo officer takes another look at your papers. You feel yourself sweating underneath your clothing and nestle up closer to the Captain who keeps badgering the officer to hurry up. "You are fine to proceed, Miss Amy Jones, you are certainly an American." The officer leaves the train and it continues on its way.

Goto **206**

482

When you leave the train the woman takes you to a cafe where you sit together talking about journalism and how to make a good story. You enjoy coffee and croissants, while she shows you pictures of places she has been. All of this talk is wearisome as it seems to be a facade but then she hands you another photograph explaining how she knew a newspaper man from Washington and points him out in the photograph. You don't recognise him but she is making such a fuss about him you decide you need to remember the face.

When you leave the cafe, she tells you that a good hotel would be the Hotel du Repose and then gives you directions to it. You follow her guidance and when you enter the lobby of the hotel, you find it to be small but quite charming. You ring the bell on the antiquated front desk and a man appears from the back. You recognise his face from the photograph and ask him if he can suggest a good room to stay in. He takes your arm and leads you out of the lobby through the kitchen.

You emerge through a back door into the alley and are bundled into a car where a blanket is placed over you as you are sped away. The journey is over an hour before you are allowed to raise your head and see where you will be staying on your mission.

Find out where at 019

483

You break one of the vials of acid in the lock and watch as the dissolving substance works its way through the mechanism. Soon the door swings open and you decide you need to brief the man on what to do next. But he doesn't give you a chance. Instead he bolts past you and straight out into the corridor. Soon you hear a commotion and there are guards everywhere searching the building. Although you manage to leave the cells you are caught trying to secret yourself in the building.

You are taken to a prison by a van and are there interrogated. For three months you endure daily questions and methods of persuasion that cause you great pain. But then one morning you are taken outside in the first rays of sun and positioned beside a wall and given a blindfold to wear. You hear a squad of soldiers being told to ready, aim and then fire. And then your war is over.

You have failed. Did you go off mission? Try again at 001.

484

You open the kitchen door and step into a substantial food preparation facility clearly designed for accommodating a large number of guests. However, as it's the middle of the night the kitchen is quiet although it is lit. There is a dumb waiter across from you, as well as a number of cupboards. You can see large ovens and a storeroom in the far corner. There is also a door in the far wall which presumably leads to the rest of the house.

Do you,

Search the cupboards – **002**

Investigate the dumb waiter – **042**

Check out the storeroom – **082**

Exit the kitchen – **200**

485

If you have arrived here, you've done something wrong because no path leads here. Go back to where you came from and pick a number that's there.

486

You tell her you left them up at the General's room and everyone looks a little embarrassed. You quickly retreat and collect them before returning out the same door where the soldier and the auxiliary simply grin as you walk past.

Good thinking and you are now free to continue with your escape. Goto **035**.

487

You watch the guard begin to walk away and run the opposite direction once you see his back turned. Unfortunately the marble floor is not good at hiding your footsteps in your auxiliary shoes and he turns back to you almost instantly. He shouts once and you don't respond. The next thing you know is that you are in pain and falling after a loud bang has split the air. After that you know nothing.

You have failed, shot down in a foreign field. Pity as you were so close. Try again at 001.

488

The chalkboard shows a single French name and two British names in cells one to three. The entry for cell four is empty. What's next in this place?

Examine the far cells – **263**

Talk to the French Peasant man – **283**

Talk to the British Pilot – **303**

489

The water becomes choppy as you clear the coast in the dinghy but soon you spot a boat in the darkness. It quickly comes alongside and you are helped aboard and taken to a small cabin. Here, the Captain congratulates you and offers you warm food and towels to dry yourself and a change of clothes. You have a journey through the night until you reach the port on the South coast of England and you fall asleep, clutching the plans to you.

As the sun rises, you come on deck and see the beautiful sight of England and safety. The day is bright and you happily watch the harbour as you arrive. On berthing a man comes on board who you recognise as the very man who sent you to France. You embrace and he heartily congratulates you. You hand over the plans and he introduces you to a colleague who will look after you while he takes the plans to those who need them.

And your job is done. You have made it, against all odds you have been a spy in France and come back alive and with German plans that will help the Allies war effort. There's no fanfare and only a debrief to look forward to but such is the life of a spy. And who knows, you may be returning in the near future.

But for now you relax and ponder all the hairy moments you escaped from, all the people who you met and the daring operations you succeeded in doing.

Welcome home, hero!

You are the Hero!

The Author

GR Jordan is a self-published author who finally decided at forty that in order to have an enjoyable lifestyle, his creative beast within would have to be unleashed. His books mirror that conflict in life where acts of decency contend with self-promotion, goodness stares in horror at evil and kindness blind-side us when we at our worst. Corrupting our world with his parade of wondrous and horrific characters, he highlights everyday tensions with fresh eyes whilst taking his methodical, intelligent mainstays on a roller-coaster ride of dilemmas, all the while suffering the banter of their provocative sidekicks.

A graduate of Loughborough University where he masqueraded as a chemical engineer but ultimately played American football, Gary had worked at changing the shape of cereal flakes and pulled a pallet truck for a living. Watching vegetables freeze at -40°C was another career highlight and he was also one of the Scottish Highlands "blind" air traffic controllers. These days he has graduated to answering a telephone to people in trouble before telephoning other people to sort it out.

Having flirted with most places in the UK, he is now based in the Isle of Lewis in Scotland where his free time is spent between raising a young family with his wife, writing, figuring out how to work a loom and caring for a small flock of chickens. Luckily his writing is influenced by his varied work and life experience as the chickens have not been the poetical inspiration he had hoped for!

Author's Notes on Female Spies in World War II France

In World War II female agents were used by the allies to work in the field for a department known as the Special Operations Executive. Set up in 1940, it amalgamated three already established secret organisations.

Only a small number of people were aware of the SOE's existence which is amazing when you consider the organisation had approximately 13,000 people in its ranks in one capacity or another. 3,200 of these people were women.

Their objectives were primarily to conduct espionage, sabotage and reconnaissance in Europe against the Axis powers and in doing so, assisted local resistance movements. France was a key area for this work.

Often the work involved operating within a circuit, a group of three persons. There was a leader who organized the group and recruited new members, a wireless operator who worked on coding and decoding, and a courier who ran messages to and from other circuits.

When hostilities had finished, the organisation was dissolved in January of 1946. The work, then done in secret, is more well-known these days but the role of the female spy is still often overlooked. Without their courage and fortitude under extreme conditions, the outcome of the war may well have been different. Like all those who served, their sacrifice and work should be understood and appreciated by the following generations.

When I was looking for subject matter for a roleplay based adventure, the idea of a spy was an easy one to think of but having read some of the stories of female undercover work in France, I felt taking on this guise for my lead character was too good to pass up. However, to write an adventure that rolls along, encompasses many different aspects of the work, and which tries to give a flavour of some of the pressures the spies were under, means that the story is probably too involved in truth for this single character. Yes, the book is meant to be enjoyable, fun and challenging, but I hope it will at least makes you curious about the work female spies of this era took part in.

A Small Request

I loved writing this adventure and I hope you enjoyed playing it. If you did please give me a large pat on the back by going to your favourite online or high street bookstore and leaving a review. Outside of delivering a freshly ground cup of coffee, this is the best way to say thanks to the author. And if you want, feel free to tell me all about your Unravel Your Destiny experience at **gary@grjordan.com**.

Look out for further Unravel Your Destiny adventures coming soon.

Notes

Feel free to make any notes you require on the following pages. There are also time checklists that you can cross off when you are in time dependent situations.

Time Check Lists

60	59	58	57	56	55	54	53	52	51
50	49	48	47	46	45	44	43	42	41
40	39	38	37	36	35	34	33	32	31
30	29	28	27	26	25	24	23	22	21
20	19	18	17	16	15	14	13	12	11
10	09	08	07	06	05	04	03	02	01

Time Out!

60	59	58	57	56	55	54	53	52	51
50	49	48	47	46	45	44	43	42	41
40	39	38	37	36	35	34	33	32	31
30	29	28	27	26	25	24	23	22	21
20	19	18	17	16	15	14	13	12	11
10	09	08	07	06	05	04	03	02	01

Time Out!

60	59	58	57	56	55	54	53	52	51
50	49	48	47	46	45	44	43	42	41
40	39	38	37	36	35	34	33	32	31
30	29	28	27	26	25	24	23	22	21
20	19	18	17	16	15	14	13	12	11
10	09	08	07	06	05	04	03	02	01

Time Out!

Notes

Notes

Notes